FALLOUT:

COOPER'S CARAVAN

Stories from the Mojave Wasteland

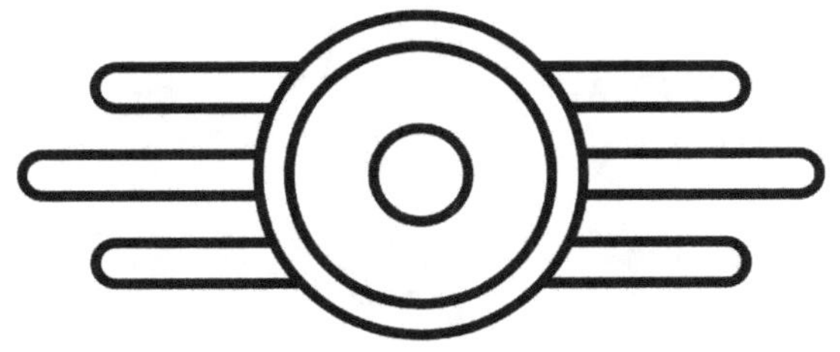

Table of Contents

I. The Plague

The ghoul plague known as "116" swept through the settlement of North Fork with the quickness and ferocity of a dying Deathclaw. It tore its way deep into the caverns cut into the side of the cliff walls of Zion where the ghouls of North Fork lived in relative quiet and peace. Insidiously, it forced its way past the normal longevity that the community of ghouls had known their entire cursed lives. The plague struck them with a sudden fear of death in a way most of the residents hadn't thought about in a long, long while. For people living so closely together, in such a remote location, it was a disaster bringing them to the brink of extinction.

In a meager room off to the side of the main cavern,

which served as the community's gathering space and dining hall, Dr. Tremain leaned over yet another new patient, listening to labored breath that was slow and raspy even by ghoul standards. He raised a cheap cigarette to his lips and lit it, the orange flicker of the lighter briefly mixing with the dull blue lights of the scavenged medical equipment. He inhaled deeply, and sighed it out. He wasn't trained at all for this kind of thing. He'd been an EMT before the Great War; he was able to patch up blown off limbs, radscorpion punctures, and other injuries common in the Wasteland, so the people of the settlement called him "Doctor," but this plague was beyond him. Ghouls don't get sick. He couldn't count the number of times he'd said and thought that over the past week, but it didn't matter. He ran a hand over his scarred face and turned around.

"Your father is in bad shape, Cooper. It's the same as the others. 116." He took another long drag on the cigarette and sighed, "I'm sorry, kid."

The tall, muscled youth standing closely behind him deflated, shoulders drooping and making him look smaller. Cooper's face, which was already creased with worry, dug in deeper. He picked a weathered coin out of the pocket of his coat and began to run it between his fingers nervously. After a minute he looked up at the doctor.

"What can we do for him?" he asked.

"For 116?" Tremain shrugged. "Nothing I've tried works for it. You could try asking one of the Followers or Canaanite missionaries at the Dead Horses camp. They did a lot of medical testing in New Canaan, I heard. Maybe they still do wherever the survivors ran off to."

"Why haven't you gone yourself?"

Tremain laughed and shook his head, "I know you haven't left the settlement much, kid, but they ain't exactly friendly to random ghouls out there in the Wastes. I'm no fighter, and anyway, I've got my hands full here."

"Then I'll go. Beyond the canyon if I have to." Cooper did his best to sound brave about it. The doctor looked like he was about to say something to protest, or to laugh, but a sudden fit of coughing from the bed stopped him. He turned back and Cooper rushed up to the bed next to him. They held their breaths.

Slowly, Cooper's father spoke. "Cooper...the Rounds...you have to...the Rounds..." Cooper took his hand, struggling to say something.

Dr. Tremain looked even more grim. "He's right, kid. Even without this goddamn plague, we're running low on plenty of other things: stims, Jet, batteries, parts for failing machinery. Someone needs to do the Rounds, and you're the only one your dad's been teaching the job to."

"Cooper..." his father began coughing again. It sounded like his lungs were climbing halfway up his throat.

"The Rounds" was an important annual event for North Fork. There wasn't much traffic coming in and out of Zion Canyon. Merchants never visited, and the only outsiders who came were the missionaries or Legion soldiers sent by Caesar. North Fork, being a small settlement of ghouls deep in a cavern, relied on the supplies brought in by their yearly caravan. They had a half-dozen aging brahmin, and the only person skilled enough in survival, bartering, and navigation was the man now lying in a makeshift bed in a dimly lit doctor's office: Thomas Pulman, Cooper's father.

The hand Cooper was holding slowly sank down out of his hand as his father slipped back into uneasy unconsciousness.

"How long does my father have?" Cooper finally asked.

"It depends. We've lost three people so far, and they all lasted no more than a month or two. Plenty more are sick. Tom here's a strong man. Decades of trips into the Wasteland haven't killed him yet, after all.

The brahmin don't move too fast, though, so I wouldn't wait around."

"Then I'll go now," said Cooper, turning to leave. He stopped at the door. "Take care of him, Doctor. Please."

Cooper walked into the main hall, which was much more quiet and empty than usual. Not even a few weeks ago, people would be sitting at the tables, playing cards, reading, listening to the radio. He'd grown up here, had birthday parties here, and seeing it without life and spirit unnerved him. No one knew how the plague moved or transmitted, so after the most recent death, people were keeping to their homes and shutting themselves away.

He walked more quickly, heading past the brahmin pen, up the scrap iron stairs and into the home he'd shared with his father up until yesterday, when he'd found him collapsed in his workshop, contents of his toolbox scattered across the floor. They were still there when Cooper walked back in and flicked on the light.

He began picking up the tools and loading them back into the box. He needed to get ready to go. Instructions, checklists, advice, admonishments, and endless lectures—half-listened to, given here in the workshop over the years—raced through his head and he tried to remember it all at once. What should he do first? What if he forgot something? Was he even ready? He squeezed his eyes shut and tried to steady his breath. He could see his father sitting on the workroom's cot, hands tinkering with something or other.

"If you forget to bring everything else, at least take a pistol and a radio. Company and protection are two things you'll need in the Wasteland."

He opened a drawer on the workbench, rummaging through screws and bits of metal, and pulled out his father's 10mm pistol. It was fit with the extended mag Cooper had modified it with just a few weeks ago in preparation for the Rounds. A sort of gift to his father. He ran his fingers along the barrel, which was polished to an oily sheen. It was heavy, and cold. Quickly, he checked the bullets and flicked the safety on before tossing it onto the cot. Grabbing the radio off a side table by the cot, he threw it into a canvas sack with the gun, the toolbox and a survival kit.

Cooper walked over to the wall and carefully removed a hand-drawn map of Zion Canyon and the surrounding area. His father had meticulously sketched it during his travels, with illustrations of plants and creatures scattered on the borders and the reverse side. A bold red line led out of the canyon and towards New Vegas, marking the path the caravan followed when doing the Rounds. Leaving the posters of blonde and busty Vault-Tec pinups where they were, Cooper folded up the map and put it gently in his shirt pocket. Before leaving the room, he grabbed his father's olive-green duster jacket. It was hooded to hide his face and full of deep pockets that jostled and jangled with a variety of mysterious implements as he moved to shut off the lights and closed the door. He grabbed some food from the kitchen, and his journal from his room. He stopped for a moment at the front door, a pack slung over his shoulder, and looked into the house that now seemed so small and empty without life in it. With a decisive movement, he shut the door and trotted down the stairs to the pen.

The six brahmin had already been loaded with the goods prepared for trade during the coming Rounds. Their combined twelve heads looked up at Cooper in unison as he approached. Pook, a rusty red brahmin younger and smaller than the others, was Cooper's favorite—he had been charged with feeding and looking after the gentle beast when he was growing up. Pook's body was freshly painted with a list of goods carried in the bulging sacks slung across its back, a sort of traveling signboard. Cooper scratched both of Pook's heads under their chins.

Usually, the departure of the caravan for the Rounds was a huge occasion in North Fork. Every year, people gave his father small gifts and charms to take with him, which he accepted warmly and with both hands. There was music and cheering. There was well-wishing and hope. The standing fluorescent lights that were usually pointed towards the ceiling of the main hall were lined up along the exit of the cavern, a simulacrum of the blinding light to be found outside the cave that Thomas Pulman, brave leader of the Rounds, would venture out into. Cooper remembered watching his father every year and feeling so proud as the lights swallowed him up for a few months. Everyone was proud.

None of that greeted Cooper as he walked the herd of brahmin towards the daylight shining at the far end of the hall. He looked over towards Dr. Tremain's office and saw him standing in the doorway, smoke curling in front of his face. He nodded at Cooper before heading back inside. Then, the caverns were as still and silent as a tomb. Reaching into his sack, he found the radio and flicked it on, catching a song just as it was ending:

"Fight, fight, fight, fight it with all of our might

Chances are some heavenly star-spangled night

We'll find out as sure as we live

Somethin's gotta give

Somethin's gotta give

Somethin's gotta give"

He walked out into the light without looking back, and put up his hood against the sun. "Come on, Pook," he said. "Let's make the Rounds."

II. The Tribe

As morning climbed towards noon, the sun was starting to come into its hot, blinding zenith, beating against the red canyon walls. Cooper squinted and raised his hand, waiting for his eyes, cloudy green and heavy with exhaustion, to adjust. He sighed and stretched tired muscles—he'd been up all night at his father's bedside. Cooper was taller than most, and well-built from all the mechanical work, scavenging, and occasional brahmin wrestling that came with being his father's apprentice. Like all ghouls, his face was a random mess of scars that looked like severe burns, and there was a flat hole where a normal human's nose would protrude. He kept his skull shaved clean, like his father had shown him.

He looked out over Zion, which was crisscrossed with muddy blue rivers, rusty plateaus, and patches of still-green trees. Far below on the floor of the canyon, a small lake sparkled, and there was a light breeze moving the hot air. Zion Canyon was spared many of the horrors of the Great War, which is why the settlement of ghouls that became North Fork originally came and made their reclusive home there. Disfigured by the blasts, they were tired of war. Zion was largely still untouched by the world outside, and most of the denizens among the wilderness here liked it that way. Aside from inter-tribal conflicts and border skirmishes with Caesar's legions, who were always seeking more land to bring under their control, the hidden canyon of Zion felt much like its own world, one Cooper had never been outside of.

Safe to say, he was a little nervous.

He felt a nudge in the small of his back and jumped, startled. It was Pook, shuffling impatiently.

"Yeah, yeah. I expect you're all ready to go. You know

the road better than I do. And you've been farther. Hopefully *you* won't get lost."

He whistled for the caravan to move, and they all started the descent down the zig-zagging path that would lead to the bottom of the canyon, and start them on the trail to the Dead Horses camp.

A sweaty hour later, Cooper stopped the caravan by the lake at the bottom to rest and have a drink. The lakes and rivers of Zion were the only place for miles and miles where the water was almost completely clean, fed by deep underground aquifers that were unaffected by the War. Clean water was one of the many things the caravan traded, half the brahmin were loaded down with tanks heavy with the stuff. Ironically, it was usually traded for irradiated water to bring back to the settlement, since the ghouls of North Fork were actually healed and strengthened by it. Sitting propped against a tree, Cooper took a swig from his canteen and looked around.

A movement. A skittering sound. The brahmin looked up and froze still, trained enough not to run, but sensing danger. He turned off the radio and listened. His heart began to pick up its pace, and when his hand found the butt of his gun in the pack, he was trembling slightly. He stood up, raising the barrel of the gun in front of him.

He was hit hard from behind, landing on his chest. He huffed out air, quickly rolling over onto his back to face his attacker, finding himself face-to-face with the many eyes and quivering mandibles of a radscorpion, its blue-black carapace reflecting brightly in the sunlight. Where had it come from? They never came to this part of the canyon. It swung a claw at him and he rolled away. Cooper reckoned the reason it was here didn't matter that much.

He gained his feet and remembered to position himself between the radscorpion and the brahmin. *Always protect the caravan. It's the settlement's lifeline.* The radscorpion made a loud, frustrated noise and charged.

Cooper fired off four quick shots towards the creature's head. Barely shaken, it barreled into Cooper and knocked him aside, heading towards the nearest brahmin. Hunger must have driven it away from its usual territory, and hunger made both man and beast desperate.

But so did survival. Cooper ran forward and threw his arms around the radscorpion's curved, lethal tail. He threw his weight to the side, pulling and twisting his body to try and throw it off course. Acidic venom dripped down off the barb, sizzling and smoking on the arm of his coat. The tail shook, but he held on, and fired another few shots at the base.

That got its attention. The radscorpion turned and faced down Cooper again. Backing up, he fired again and again, but the creature was still coming.

Stand your ground. Plant your feet, and slow down. Focus, and take aim. Find a weak point.

A weak point. For the radscorpions, where was it? He

dodged as the creature charged again, splashing into the water's edge. This was his opening. It was weakened. He brought the pistol up, took a deep breath, and things slowed down. He looked over the creature. Face, body, tail, legs, claws. The claws! They were sensitive! With this pistol, with how far away it was, he had a decent chance of hitting them. He unloaded the rest of his clip, and they shredded apart under the barrage of bullets. The radscorpion reared up, screeched, and fell down, twitching in the water.

Cooper was breathing heavily. That had certainly been more intense than shooting at cans or birds outside the cave. Still, he felt a bit more sure of the gun in his hand, and a bit better about shooting overall. He began to walk over towards the herd to check on them, brushing himself off, when he stopped.

Radscorpions often traveled in groups, and the rest of them had arrived. Cooper was surrounded, and his gun was empty. He looked over to the tree, where his bag and ammo were, just in time to see another large scorpion step over top of it on its way towards him.

This wasn't good. Reaching into one of the pockets on his father's coat, he pulled out and unsheathed a carving knife. Better than nothing. He gripped it tightly and backed towards Pook, trying to look everywhere at once.

Shots rang out. Echoing off the canyon walls and making it impossible to tell how many and from where they were coming. Within seconds, the group of scorpions were all lying dead on the ground, and the brahmin went back to drinking.

"What the—?" Cooper didn't put away his knife.

"*Hoi*, Thomas!" came a voice, and Cooper saw a man slide down from his perch up on the rocks. He slung a battered rifle over his shoulder and smiled. "Can't believe seeing you in such danger. And how many shots missed? Finally getting old, *ahk iss*? Ha!"

As the man ran up, Cooper recognized him as Two-Bears, one of the Dead Horse tribe's warriors who usually spent his time outside the camp, not so much hunting as shooting whatever he came across that he didn't like or looked edible. He used to chase Cooper around, laughing and making Yao Guai noises, to entertain the child when his father was doing business. His face was covered in swirling tattoos and an ever-present toothy grin.

"Two-Bears! Great timing!" Cooper threw back his hood.

"Cooper? Gods! A surprise, but a *good* surprise. What are you doing, Small-One?"

Cooper's words tumbled out too quickly. "My father's sick. Dying. The whole settlement is. It's just me and a few others, so I'm--"

"On the Rounds, yes? A big journey for Cooper Pulman. Not ready. You will need help." In his quick, decisive manner, he turned and began striding off, "Come, come." He gave Pook a pat on the left-head as he passed by.

Cooper grabbed his pack and whistled to signal the caravan to start moving. As he passed by the downed radscorpions, he stopped to cut off the ends of the tails, where the poison gland was, throwing them into a pack that had space on one of the brahmin. *Take whatever can be sold or traded*, his father's voice said in his mind.

As they walked to the Dead Horses camp, Cooper described the dire situation of North Fork to Two-Bears. He didn't know about the plague, but could sense the worry in Cooper and did his best to reassure him before turning to stories of recent hunts, including his recent successful theft of a Legionary's helmet from one of Caesar's scouting patrols.

The late afternoon sun was on its way down as they arrived, and the Dead Horse encampment was cool and shady. Cooper heard excitement as his caravan was spotted, and then confusion as his father was not seen. Two-Bears turned to him.

"I will speak to Joshua Graham. Knows about outside places. Stay here. Talk. Rest. Sell your wares, Rounds-Walker." He winked and smiled before running off towards the steps that led up to the leader's base above the camp.

People were watching him, looking at him and his caravan over. Two-Bears, not being exactly in line with things like custom, had always called Cooper's father Thomas, but 'Rounds-Walker' is what the tribe had always called him. Cooper couldn't help but feel a little proud, important. He stood straighter and put on a loud performance voice, as his father used to, letting the familiarity of the routine chase away some of his worry and fear.

"*Yah ah tahg*! Come, come! See the wares of North Fork! We proudly buy, sell, and trade with the people of Dead Horse! We come here first to bring the best to our dear friends!"

They began to walk over, looking over the brahmin and poking around in the bags. For over an hour,

Cooper shook hands, bartered, argued, inspected, smiled, and plied his trade. One older man was especially reluctant to let go of a shiny piece of circular metal that Cooper recognized straightaway as a locking mechanism for the kind of doors North Fork used for their storage rooms. Unlike many of his Dead Horse tribesmen, the old man didn't speak even the smallest amount of English (except the word 'No,' which he seemed to know well, or enjoy practicing). Through a combination of hand gestures, dirt drawings, and a little help from another customer, Cooper was able to make a good deal for it, and smiled at his accomplishment. He was also able to get his hands on more 10mm ammo for his pistol, a few books, some sensor modules, and a number of tanned hides that his father said always sold well outside the canyon.

The business proceedings were suddenly interrupted. "Cooper Pulman! Son of Thomas! Let us speak!" Joshua Graham's voice carried over the crowd from above, and all was quiet in his presence. The tribesmen nodded at Cooper and motioned him towards the steps. He let the brahmin be led away towards a nearby pen. He could trust the Dead Horses. Graham, he was less sure about.

He had met Joshua Graham only once before during a quick trip into the Dead Horse camp a few years back. Aside from the Rounds, his father made smaller trips around Zion Canyon for local trading, gossip, and what he called "ghoul outreach" with a wry half-smile. Cooper sometimes accompanied him on those, as part of his training and also because his father could do nothing to dissuade his eagerness for getting out of the cave. Graham mostly concerned himself with the tribe's military matters, leaving economics to the locals, but this one time he had come down to speak to Cooper's father in hushed tones. Cooper had been uneasy around the bandaged man, whose hard, gray eyes were the only thing visible beneath the layers of wrapping. He had heard Graham called the Burned Man (although never when the man was within earshot), and heard tales of his bloodthirsty military campaigning and ruthless tactics.

Despite the day's small successes in combat and trade, Cooper was still uneasy in his presence now, years later. This compounded his surprise at the warm tone in Graham's gravelly voice.

"Welcome, Cooper. Please, sit," he motioned to a bench on one side of the table, on which lay rows of guns. Cooper recognized most of them as .45 Autos, the chosen weapon of the New Canaanites. Graham saw Cooper looking them over and laughed, picking one up and beginning to clean it. "If you are admiring our arms, you have good taste. Your father also had a keen eye for weaponry," he paused, "I was...sorry to hear about his condition."

"You were friends with my father?" asked Cooper.

"I have a great respect for Thomas Pulman, who has done much to keep peace and promote civility in this place. I suspect many others feel the same. He is a good, strong man. Faithful, in his own way. So, what would you ask of me?"

"I need to find a cure to the plague called 116. Do you know it?"

"Not specifically, I'm afraid." Graham saw Cooper's face fall, "However, if there's a sickness that can affect ghouls, I do know who would be studying it. They may have your answers."

"Who? Where? I'll do whatever it takes." Desperation lay thick in Cooper's voice, making him sound even younger than he was, and contrasting with Graham's demeanor, which was heavy and smooth like a vault door. It was with that same heaviness and authority that he spoke:

"'Give, and it shall be given unto you; good measure, pressed down, and shaken together, and running over, shall men give into your bosom. For with the same measure that ye mete with it shall be measured to you again.' Book of Luke, Chapter 6, Verse 38."

Cooper had heard his father talk about the New Canaanites' holy book. Mostly he said to be very careful about it. His father had also warned Cooper about his sharp tongue and penchant for jokes, which amused his neighbors, but could get him into trouble on the road, especially with a man like Graham. With some effort, he kept his mouth shut and his eyes locked with Graham's, who seemed to be considering Cooper much in the same way he looked over his arsenal of weaponry.

"Your father's business, now your business, is one of trade. I will give you information and assistance, but I will require an equal amount of...value from you. I ask because it is necessary, and because in this way we can help one another."

"What do you need?" Cooper asked without hesitation.

Graham picked up one of the pistols from the table, and leveled it at the wall. "These pistols were created hundreds of years ago by one of my tribe. Learning how to handle one is an important tradition to the New Canaanites. Traditions, shared history, are what keep a tribe alive, even if the body is destroyed, even if the land is lost, traditions survive. When New Canaan fell to the White Legs, sinners striking from the darkness at Caesar's command, they tried to steal part of that tradition, turning our own weapons against us."

Graham took a deep breath and released his tightening grip on the pistol, placing it on the table. "These weapons here are what I have recovered over the years. I had been stockpiling them for war, but with the White Legs now driven from Zion, they have had their retribution. I recently learned of a group of New Canaanites seeking to rebuild, and would see these guns returned to my people so that they can continue our traditions. The doctor you seek can be found with them, in a hospital north-east of New Vegas."

Aside from a pistol for protection, weapons were not taken on the Rounds. It was one of his father's rules, as part of his efforts to keep North Fork out of any conflict. He also said that deadly tools tended to attract deadly attention, and arms-dealing was more trouble than it was worth. Yet, with no other leads to go on, Cooper didn't see he had much of a choice.

"I'll take them," he replied after a minute, meeting Graham's gaze, "What's the name of the doctor?"

There was no way to tell for sure under the bandages, but something in Graham's eyes looked as if he smiled for the briefest of moments. "Doctor Micah. I will mark the hospital's location on your map. May you find the path you seek, young Cooper, and remember that there is a light at the end of all darkness."

They loaded up a crate with the .45 Autos, gleaming black like radscorpion tails in the afternoon sun, and with just as much dormant potential for quick death. When Cooper shut the lid he looked up and saw that Graham was handing one more gun to him. He spoke.

"*Avenge not yourselves, but rather give place unto wrath: for it is written, Vengeance is mine; I will repay, saith the*

Lord.'" He pressed the weapon into Cooper's hand, "Should you come across any of Caesar's dogs on your path to the truth, repay them with this for me."

When Cooper made it back to the brahmin pen, he saw Two-Bears sitting atop one of the fence posts. He leaped off and strode towards Cooper.

"Joshua Graham helped?" he asked.

"Yeah, he did," said Cooper. "I need to go out of the canyon, to a hospital north of New Vegas."

"You will go Outside? To the City of Lights?" Two-Bears looked concerned, and then clearly settled something. "I will take you to the Outside. We go now. Climb before dark." Again, he strode off without consulting or confirming with Cooper. He thought about protesting, but he had finished his business at the settlement, and he was, without question, in a rush. He opened the pen and whistled for the caravan to continue, strapping the heavy case of Canaanite guns to the back of one of the brahmin. He did not update the painted sign on its hide, as he had with the day's other recent trades.

Walking after Two-Bears, Cooper reached into his sack and flicked the radio back on. A few sad-sounding bars on the harmonica, and then a group of voices slowly sang:

In the shadow of the valley

I would like to settle down

Wide open space

Wind on my face

A distant horizon

The moon on the crest

In the shadow of the valley

That I love best

You have always waited for me

And you always will be there

Sagebrush and pine

Old friends of mine

A little bit further

I will find my rest

In the shadow of the valley

That I love best

III. The Outside

The way leading out of the Dead Horses camp climbed up to the edge of the canyon towards New Vegas, and was littered with booby traps, pitfalls, and a variety of hidden dangers that would take even a skilled outsider hours to work through without losing a finger or two. This was all to keep back Caesar's troops, who still held something of an ongoing vendetta against Joshua Graham and the tribe that took him in, and whose recent losses compelled them to seek territory that was outside NCR control. Every once in a while, patrols would try and make their way down towards the lights of the camp, perhaps hoping to impress Caesar with new discoveries, only to turn a corner and discover a bear trap—one without an auto-rigged shotgun if they were lucky. Two-Bears thought it unlikely they'd run into any Legionaries, humming merrily as he picked his way past the deadly traps, deftly disarming them so the caravan could safely pass through. "I reset later," he said offhandedly.

"If you remember," Cooper replied with a smile. Two-Bears laughed and nodded, still unworried. The radio had switched to news, talking about increased activity on the outskirts of The Strip, making it harder for people to get in and out. Two-Bears made a sound, and requested the radio be changed to something with music. Cooper obliged, fiddling with the dial until it settled on cheery, jaunty music wholly unfitting to their dangerous trek up the side of a trap-filled canyon.

Oh, I got spurs that jingle, jangle, jingle

I got spurs that jingle, jangle, jingle

Two-Bears turned around, grinning. "Ya!" he shouted, and began to sing along, acting as both lead singer and repeating chorus:

As I go ridin' merrily along

"As I go ridin' merrily along"

And they sing, "Oh, ain't you glad you're single?"

"And they sing, 'Oh, ain't you glad you're single?'"

And that song ain't so very far from wrong

"And that song ain't so very far from wrong"

His singing voice was better than Cooper would have imagined, and Two-Bears lost all trace of his accent when singing. Cooper soon found himself joining in, and they finished the song together, laughing, as Two-Bears stooped down to gently detach a wire rigged to a pump-action shotgun at waist-level. Cooper found that he was smiling for what felt like the first time in a while. He took a deep breath and looked up at the sky, where the sun was on its way towards setting. Had he really left just this morning? When was the last time he'd slept?

They continued walking up the canyon, bopping and humming along to the music until they reached the top. The sun was now properly setting, and the vast desert plains of the Mojave Wasteland stretched out as far as they could see, lit up in reds, yellows, and oranges.

"Welcome, Small-One Cooper Pulman, son of Thomas and new Rounds-Walker, to Outside," said Two-Bears, stepping up beside him. "Is for tomorrow. Wasteland darkness is many dangers." He pointed to an outcrop of rocks further along the edge of the canyon. "*Roo too nait, ahk iss.* Tonight we sleep."

They set up camp in a small alcove among the rocks as it was getting dark. After getting the brahmin settled and watered, Cooper climbed up to the top of the tallest rock and looked out. On the distant horizon, he thought that he could just make out the glittering neon lights of The Strip. It could have just as easily been a large Raider encampment, for all Cooper knew. He'd never been out of the canyon. This was as far as he'd been from North Fork, and he had a lot farther to go. Looking at the vast expanse of darkness that was the rest of the world, Cooper didn't feel fear at the dangers undoubtedly lurking there, but excitement at seeing it all for himself, and testing his mettle against whatever he found.

He climbed back down and sat next to Two-Bears, who had started a fire and was holding a skewer of meats over it. "Gecko. Is *goot*," he said by way of explanation, offering one to Cooper. Immediately, he shoved half the stick into his mouth, his brain being too slow to stop his exhausted, hungry body from burning the roof of his mouth. He must have made a funny sight waving his hands frantically into his mouth to cool it off, because Two-Bears howled with laughter. They sat and quietly ate for a while before he spoke up, "Cooper, what asked Joshua Graham to you?"

Cooper explained his agreement with Graham to deliver the guns and Graham's personal request that Cooper shoot any Legionary troops he saw on sight. An excited look, like a man coming home to a table full of dinner, flashed by Two-Bears' eyes. Cooper upholstered and held up the .45 Auto that Graham had given him for the task. Two-Bears held out his hand for it, and Cooper gave it to him for inspection. He looked it up and down, nodding in approval. "We can kill many Legion *Owslanders* with this. Cooper will keep promise to Joshua Graham."

"*Owslanders...*" Cooper pondered over the Res word the tribes used for outsiders beyond the canyon walls. "Aren't my father and I, the people of North Fork, outsiders too?"

"*Vass*? No no!" Two-Bears' eyes widened in surprise at the thought, "Cooper, Thomas Pulman, tribe of North Fork are all *nachkbar*." He paused for a moment while he thought of the English word for it. Most of the English Two-Bears knew was from music on the radio or the traders he came across. "*Nayybers, ya?*" he pronounced it as a word still foreign to him, "Good people of the canyon. Trade, share. Don't attack."

Cooper smiled, "Yeah, I guess we are neighbors. Thank you, Two-Bears, for coming with me."

Two-Bears clapped a heavy hand on Cooper's shoulder, "Is what *nachkbar* do. I will help. My gun with yours." He threw the .45 Auto back to Cooper. "Excited? First times to battle with Legion, Raiders, feral ghouls—ah, sorry." Two-Bears looked a bit shamefaced at the last one, forgetting his present company.

"I don't know, actually," said Cooper, looking into the fire. "Killing people seems...different from killing radroaches and bloatflies, you know?"

"Is different, *ya*," said Two-Bears after a moment. "It's more like killing Yao Guai. Or Night Stalker. Want to kill *you* first. Will try very hard. Remember to do that. Man with a gun," he leveled his own rifle at Cooper, who flinched but didn't move or break eye contact, "is more dangerous than animals of Wasteland. Man with a gun and mission, or fear, or both...he is most dangerous. You," he shook the rifle at Cooper, "be more dangerous. Survive."

Two-Bears lowered the rifle and finished eating. He

stood up and looked out into the darkness beyond their campsite. Cooper put the pistol down on a rock next to him and walked over to where he was standing, looking out with him. Two-Bears' eyes were focused on the distance, but seemed to be looking somewhere else. When he spoke, it was more quiet and serious than Cooper usually heard him.

"Was much fighting in the canyon. Long ago...before Cooper. Fighting between tribes. Attacks from Caesar and other *owslanders*. Much killing. Fires. *Koh bambuh*—bombings—many things lost. Town of New Canaan gone. Women, children, all killed. Dead Horses were afraid. Weak. White Legs had *owslander* weapons. Wanted to take everything. Joshua Graham taught us to fight. To protect *Landinetah*—our land— keep balance, defend what is important. Your father..."

Two-Bears stopped, then seemed to make a decision, "Your father brought Joshua Graham to canyon. Brought guns to Dead Horses. Fought with us to keep the canyon safe. Sometimes, I have to fight. Have to kill. Or lose everything to man who can. This is what means *hozho abwagen*. Good, evil in...heart's balancing." Two-Bears' pointed to his chest, then made a frustrated look of concentration. "Is difficult in English. Next time we is meeting, Cooper is learning speak Res."

At this, Cooper laughed in an exhale from a breath he didn't know he was holding. His father didn't speak much about his past and the things he did outside the canyon. Thinking of him in a full-scale battle alongside the likes of Joshua Graham, facing down Caesar's Legionaries or savage White Leg warriors...it didn't fit at all with the same man who made shadow puppet shows from the light of his workbench to help a young Cooper get to sleep; or who mediated fights and arguments in the settlement, insisting on peace over conflict. *There are no winners in fights unless peace is found at the end.* His head was full of questions. He opened his mouth to try and work through the long list of them when Two-Bears held up a hand, silencing him.

"*Sist!* Listen." Two-Bears scanned the darkness, inhaling deeply through his nose as he did. Cooper couldn't see, or smell, anything. The only sound was the low crackling of the campfire behind them. He strained his eyes into the night, imaging that, just maybe, he saw some movement out ahead…

Two-Bears tackled him to the ground just as gunfire erupted, loudly ricocheting off the stones around them and sending shards into the air. "*Shaiss*! Cooper! Go!" They both scrambled low along the sand, sharp rocks digging into palms and knees, bullets hitting all around them. There was a small break in the onslaught and Two-Bears dragged them behind a large boulder just as more shots rang out. Cooper reached for his holster and Two-Bears to his back at the same time, both grasping for guns that weren't there. Now, above the gunfire, Cooper could hear voices shouting from multiple directions.

Two-Bears looked at Cooper and pointed to the

campfire. "Get rifle! Will come back!" he stood up, let off a loud war cry, and ran off through the stones. More shouting, and the shooting moved away in the direction Two-Bears had run in. Cooper dashed to the ring of rocks around the fire, which had burned low, barely giving off any light. He grabbed the .45 Auto and swung Two-Bears' rifle over his back, running off in the direction he had gone.

He saw the first attacker from behind. Polished metal armor glinting in the moonlight, which meant Legionaries. Cooper hoped that the gun Joshua Graham had given him could go through whatever armor the Legion wore. Heart beating loudly in his ears, Cooper aimed and squeezed off two shots, which seemed so much louder, and kicked harder in his hands than his father's 10mm pistol. The man fell down face-first into the sand, sparing Cooper having to see his face as he ran by.

He emerged from between two boulders, then threw himself backwards just in time to avoid a flurry of shots from his left. A voice shouted, "Halt! In the name of Caesar!" Cooper waited and stooped low, taking a deep breath before leaning out from the rock and taking aim. The .45 Auto's luminescent sights threw a green dot into the middle of the Legionary's chest, and Cooper fired off three quick shots just as the man was swinging his gun downward towards Cooper's position. There was a cry of pain, and he saw the man fall backwards, his submachine gun spraying a few rounds into the surroundings. Cooper ran forward and stood over him for a moment. In the darkness, it was hard to make out his face. Sudden movement snapped his attention back to where he was, and he looked up just in time to see three more run into view. They swept the area with freshly lit torches and spotted him. Two Legionaries armed with guns started firing, while the third, wielding a red and gold shield and raising a gleaming silver machete over his head, started running full tilt in Cooper's direction. Cooper fired a few shots, but it did nothing to slow the charging Legionary down, either going wild or glancing off the shield. The

.45 Auto clicked on an empty magazine, so he turned and ran, weaving past rocks, shouts and stomping footfalls following him closely behind.

He turned a corner into an alley between rock walls and soon found himself boxed in. A dead end. He swore under his breath and began to search through the pockets of his coat, his hands settling on the familiar weight of his father's 10mm pistol. It was less powerful, but it'd have to do. Torches appeared at the end of the alley. *Focus, and take aim. Find a weak point.* His father's words echoed in his head as he gripped the pistol and looked down the sights at the advancing soldier wielding the machete (because, honestly, he'd rather be shot than get anywhere near that blade). Sensing trapped prey, the Legionaries had slowed down and were moving carefully. Cooper had heard that Caesar's Legion took prisoners in raids, using the conquered as slaves.

"Will need to hit hole for face in helmet." Two-Bears said as he dropped down next to him. He took his rifle off of Cooper's back and readied it. "Thank you for holding."

"Two-Bears! I was worried you'd left me here!"

"No no. Defend what's important, *ya*? Now, fire!"

With the sudden appearance of another enemy, the Legionary with the machete began charging again. Two-Bears fired his rifle, and the Legionary stumbled, slowing down and clutching his leg. Cooper raised his pistol, focused, and could clearly see the space between the gaps in the helmet. He fired a single shot that tore straight through the center, and the Legionary's face exploded into red mist that was only somewhat contained by his helmet. Taking Two-Bears' lead, Cooper then aimed for the exposed legs of the next soldier, getting a few shots in. Two-Bears finished him off, leaving only the last one, who had taken cover behind a low rock. Two-Bears fired a couple shots across the rock before reloading. The man popped out to fire, but Cooper sent another bullet through his helmet, too. Things were quiet for a moment after the combat, until Two-Bears turned to Cooper mid-reload and yelled, "Hahaha! *Goot keel, ahk iss*! Very good!"

Two-Bears trotted forward to where the first downed soldier lay, picking up his torch. "To the Four Winds they go. Come, Cooper." As they worked through the bodies, looting mostly ammo and Legion coinage, Two-Bears recounted how he had led off half the group, leaving one alive long enough to question him about their mission in the area. They were sent as a forward scouting party for a local Legate, one of Caesar's warlords. More troops were going to be coming into the canyon, seeking to gain more territory and to raid any groups they found there.

"I will go back," he said. "To warn Joshua Graham of this. I am sorry."

"I was afraid of that, but I understand. Thank you, Two-Bears, for coming with me this far. It was...nice."

"*Dank ni*, Cooper Pulman. Most fun in long time. Next time, we go together."

As they were heading back to the campfire, they passed by the first Legionary that Cooper had killed, the man he had shot in the back. Two-Bears stopped them and looked at Cooper. "This first kill?" Cooper nodded. Two-Bears flipped the man over and began digging through his pockets and armor, looking for something. "Ah," he said, holding up something that dangled and spun on the end of a chain. He handed it to Cooper, who held it into the light of the torch. It was a golden medallion, with the words *Audentes Fortuna Iuvat* inscribed in a circle around a pair of wings. It must have laid against the Legionary's chest somewhere near where Cooper had shot him, because the lower edge was darkened with blood.

"What does it say?" he asked Two-Bears.

Two-Bears shrugged. "Don't read. And don't speak Legion-language. But, it is important to take this thing. A first kill you must remember and carry. Learn. Move forward. Be strong and kill when you have to, but keep balance." He poked a finger into Cooper's chest.

Two-Bears showed Cooper how to restart the fire with a set of sharp stones that he kept in a pouch. Once it was going, he handed the pouch to Cooper, smiling.

"Are you looking to sell it? I am a trader, after all." Cooper gestured to the brahmin, who had obediently stayed in place during the whole skirmish—how much gunfire had they heard over the year with his father? Cooper shook away the thought and smiled. "I also, uh, recently acquired some Legion money."

Two-Bears laughed, "*Dank ni*, but no. Is gift. For The Rounds. Be safe, Cooper Pulman." They clasped hands, and Two-Bears ran off into the darkness back the way they had come. He was soon out of sight, and Cooper was alone again. He sat down heavily by the fire. Despite the number of times he'd almost been injured or killed, Cooper actually felt pretty good, more experienced. *"Learn. Move forward."* Two-Bears had said, and he had definitely learned. Tomorrow, he would move forward.

For now, he was exhausted. He had been ready to sleep shortly after his gecko-meat dinner, but now that the adrenaline in his system had calmed down, he could barely keep his eyes open. He took off his coat and rolled it up into a lumpy makeshift pillow, then took the radio out of his bag, lying down next to the fire and turning it on. It was nice to hear something other than the lonely Wasteland night.

Stars of the midnight ranges

Shining through the night

Stars of the midnight ranges

Light my way tonight

While my herd is grazin'

Guide them til the dawn

Watch them while I'm sleepin'

Till the stars are gone

IV. The Boomers

Cooper encountered his first official customers the next morning. He had left the outcropping of rocks at the canyon's edge and headed in the direction of New Vegas after an over-long sleep, and it was only a few hours before he caught sight of a small group of travelers. They waved him down and Cooper approached cautiously, hood covering most of his face and his hand on the holster of his pistol. It turned out not to be necessary, as the group consisted of two families with children. Cooper had considered using an intimidating approach, but the children had never seen a ghoul before, and their barrage of blunt, wide-eyed questions served to make the whole situation light in tone and absurdly funny.

"Are you like a skeleton under there?"

"Can I smell you?"

"Can you talk to monsters?"

"Do you turn feral at the full moon?"

"Do you like cereal?"

"Where'd your nose go?"

The adults minding the group were mortified, but their protests and reprimands did nothing to stem the tide of questions that Cooper struggled to keep up with while conducting business. Their interview continued throughout the trade deals, Cooper jokingly answering here or there as he bartered for decent prices on some water and canned goods he was carrying, which the travelers were running low on. He found out through their conversation that they were fleeing fresh fighting south of the Hoover Dam, hoping to find a quiet settlement somewhere further north. They also gave a bit more information about the settlement of New

Canaanites setting up outside of New Vegas, which they had heard about from one of the missionaries working with The Followers. They were going to try and start a new town with others who would be coming later. Cooper asked why they didn't just take their chances with the well-established civilization under Caesar's Legion or the NCR. The oldest in the group, a stocky man with an iron-gray beard and pale-blue eyes, gave an answer that Cooper found himself repeating in his head throughout the rest of the day.

"It's the children. The only thing that matters is that they have a future and a home. Everything we have and know, it'll get passed on to them someday, and if we can teach them how to make things better in this world, it keeps hope for something brighter when we're gone. They're a fresh start. They're our life after death."

Cooper finished his dealings with the families and waved goodbye, realizing as the children joyfully called out "Bye, Mr. Ghoul, sir!" that the whole encounter marked his first time interacting with strangers outside the canyon, save the few he had killed the night before. This had been nicer. Absentmindedly, he scratched at the flat, scarred space of skin where his nose should have been, then whistled for the caravan to move on.

The next few days passed by slowly, with nothing interrupting the constant pace of the caravan save for a few small radscorpions and some coyotes that Cooper made quick work of with his pistols. He tried to limit his stops, and the only other people he encountered were a pair of Brotherhood of Steel guards patrolling Route 15, who poked through his possessions and charged him a road toll ("For keeping it free of Deathclaws and Khans, you know?"). He hadn't heard of the Brotherhood coming this far south before, but things had been on the move recently. He paid the toll, as all caravans were expected to, and walked on until dark.

As the sun went down, he could now clearly see the

neon lights of the New Vegas Strip. Sitting in the middle of the desert as it did, it was something of a miracle to Cooper's eyes, which had only ever known the harsh fluorescent lights that barely illuminated the caves of North Fork. Colors danced and changed, and the whole city seemed completely untouched by the night around it. It existed almost in its own world, one so totally different from the pristine nature of Zion. It had barely been a week since he had left the canyon, and yet the things he'd seen and done felt greater and bigger than the sum of all the years before them. He wanted to know that city and the people there. He wanted to match his skills against theirs and come back with more supplies than the brahmin could carry. He wanted to succeed, not just for his father's survival or that of the settlement, but so that he could come back into this world again and again. Tomorrow, he would enter the city and do everything he had to do, and then he'd go north and find a cure for 116.

Cooper set up his camp facing the bright lights of New

Vegas, laying on his side so he could stare at it until a comfortable, satisfied sleep washed over him. In his dreams, he was leading the caravan down multicolored streets, the walls of skyscrapers reaching endlessly into a starlit sky, followed by a parade of people with faces full of smiles and hands full of money.

Sleeping as happily and fitfully as he was, Cooper didn't so much as stir when a pair of hands pressed a wet rag over his mouth and nose, only waking briefly to see a masked face looming over him before the fumes of the chemical mixture soaked into the rag dragged him down into something deeper than sleep.

Moments of waking came through the darkness like lightning flashes across a pitch-black night, and mixed with vivid dreams.

A white-hot sun beating down from a cloudless sky.

Voices from a radio, then laughter.

A line of trees, perfectly straight.

The frayed green canvas of the cot in his father's workshop.

Walls made of grids of wire and metal.

Flashing neon lights spelling Gomorrah in flickering fire-like orange.

A baby crying on the ground, covered in blood and ash.

A man in a gas mask whistling as he cleans a rifle.

People stooped over and ran between tents, arms full of meager possessions.

A woman lying on the ground, cradling a bundle in her arms, flames around her.

His father's face, kind and reassuring.

An iron chest, closed and latched shut.

Brahmin painted with colorful letters spelling "Happy Birthday"

Mountains pushing themselves out of the desert before lifting off into the sky.

A ruined aircraft, upside down and rusting, piloted by

skeletal figures.

A bright flash like a second sun—bodies tossed aside like discarded trash.

His own face, smooth and whole, slowly falling apart.

Then, a long period of pulsating blackness, beating like the inside of a heart.

Cooper began to swim towards consciousness from the deep waters of his drug-induced dreams. He could hear raised voices, and became aware of a body that was maybe his being shaken by the shoulders.

"Hey! Come on now! Zombie sleep time is over!"

The world poured back into Cooper's senses all at once, rushing in an overwhelming wave. He could feel the hands gripping his arms, but his first, panicked thoughts were of the caravan and its precious cargo. Stronger than he looked, Cooper threw his feet into the chest of the man hovering over him, sending him tumbling off the cart and into the dirt. He stood up too fast, and his vision clouded and blurred once again as he heard shouts. Someone grabbed him, and he threw them off immediately. He reached out to brace himself on something, but his hands grasped only air and he went to his knees again. When his vision cleared, he saw a group of men and women surrounding him, all armed with heavy assault rifles. He put his hands up and tried to speak.

"Wuh..." was the most that he managed before he was grabbed by several sets of hands. His own were forced behind his back and bound together.

"Alright, alright. Let's go," said a voice by his ear. "Got me right in the chest, too. Damn shufflers. Probably half-feral."

Cooper was shoved forward as the group started to walk. For the first time, he looked around to see where he was. Huge iron artillery cannons pointed out towards the Wasteland from inside a tall wire fence. There were squat, gray buildings with people moving heavy crates between them, and guards with missile launchers standing watch in lookout towers. His heavily-armed escorts, walking closely on either side with a hand clasped firmly on Cooper's arms, wore thick black jackets over blue coveralls.

"Where are we going?" Cooper ventured, but got no response. "Chatty bunch," he mused before slipping back into watchful silence. His holster that held the .45 Auto from Joshua Graham was empty, but he was still wearing his overcoat, which meant the 10mm might still be in his pocket. He looked sideways at the weapons his kidnappers were carrying—what appeared to be customized and exceedingly well-maintained Marksman carbines, with a camouflage finish instead of the standard dull black. Military issue, probably. As a fan of high-quality hardware, Cooper was impressed, but as a current captor, he was somewhat discouraged. He decided to keep walking and see where the group was taking him.

They turned past a building that said "Schoolhouse," and Cooper could see small, curious faces peering out of the window at him as he passed by. They came up to a heavy wooden door and the guard to his left knocked before entering. The space inside consisted of a large main room that was furnished with couches, rugs, and plenty of bookshelves. It looked homey in a way that none of the scrapped together rooms in North Fork did, and it was completely at odds with the heavy fortifications outside. An old woman with her silver hair pulled back into a tight bun came out of a back room carrying a tray bearing a teapot and cups. She spoke as she set it down on the table.

"Well, now, I don't think the restraints were necessary for our guest here," she chided. "Get him untied and let him have a seat so we can talk comfortably."

The guards fussed with the ropes behind Cooper's back and soon his hands were free. He went to massage his wrists when he noticed his left arm was wrapped in metal plating up to his elbow. It was unremarkable and featureless, save a domed red light just below his hand. He went to pull on it when the old woman spoke up,

"I wouldn't mess with that too much, child. It's quite a sensitive device." She gestured to the couch adjacent to her, and placed a freshly poured cup in front of it. Warily, Cooper sat down. The old lady sipped at her tea and waved at the guards by the door, "And a little privacy for us, too, thank you." The guards nodded, left, and closed the door quietly.

"That's better," she said.

"Who are you?" was the first question of the many Cooper could think to ask.

"Oh my, you are absolutely right, child. My apologies! My name is Pearl. Welcome to our community. The outsiders call us Boomers, which we like just fine."

There was that word again: outsiders. Cooper had heard of the Boomers, namely that they didn't interact or trade with anyone beyond their walls, and in fact usually blew up anyone who tried. Cooper's father had steered clear of their territory, not wanting to join the half-dozen unlucky caravans that had wandered a bit too close and gotten shelled by artillery. To his knowledge, no one had ever been inside their heavily fortified base, despite plenty of attempts from those looking to raid their vast stores of munitions and weapons. Their compound was a treasure trove of valuable machines, generators, and more. Things North Fork could certainly use, although he didn't know what he had in the packs that these Boomers might want to trade for, or if they were remotely interested in trade.

A horrified thought sprang into Cooper's mind. "The brahmin! Where's the caravan of brahmin?" He stood up, but Pearl gently grabbed his hand.

"Calm yourself, child. They are safe here in the compound, as are all the goods carried with them. They were transported together with you. We are not raiders, and have no need for stealing."

Cooper sat back down. "Why did you bring me here, then? And why did you knock me out? And what's this thing on my arm?" he asked, all in the same breath.

"I'll explain, but please do help yourself to some tea." Cooper had actually never had tea before. He figured if the Boomers were going to kill him, they had plenty of opportunity aside from poison tea. He sipped at it and found it bitter and tasting a bit like roots and grass. The ghouls sometimes had coffee, beer, and other, stronger drinks during special occasions in North Fork. Cooper had tried alcohol for the first time at his birthday the year before, but that had made his head feel a little lighter and fuzzy, whereas the tea was clearing his mind and sharpening it. He made a face, but drank the rest of the cup.

"It's brewed from ingredients we grow and forage around here. Broc flowers, xander root, and a few other things. Do you like it? It keeps the mind ready and the body awake. It's good for important work and long journeys, which leads me to why you're here, child." She set down her cup and refilled it along with Cooper's.

She took a sip and began to talk. "We've been here for

over 50 years, and in that time we've tried to hold onto our history while shaping our own futures. So much in the world outside has changed—is always changing, but we haven't. We've kept here to ourselves so that we can be in control of our own story. That's why we have the museum and the mural, and that's why we have Pete, the Keeper of the Story. Well, we *had* him, up until a month ago, when he was taken from us."

"That sounds like a real tragedy, but where do I fit into this 'story'?" The tea hadn't completely relieved Cooper's headache, and was actually starting to make him feel a little jittery and impatient, as he became aware of time slipping away from his urgent business and an impending sense that he was about to be thrown way off track.

"Am I about to be thrown way off track?" he asked aloud before he realized it.

Pearl gave him a patient smile, and continued. "We heard word that the ghoul caravan out of Zion Canyon was setting out for his usual trade route—we may not do business with outsiders, but we do keep an eye on things, you realize. I had some of our men go out to...retrieve you. I admit I didn't specify how they should bring you here, and some of them are a bit paranoid when it comes to outsiders coming this way."

"Wasn't exactly a comfortable ride," Cooper mumbled.

"I imagine not, and I do apologize, child." Pearl placed her hand on top of Cooper's, and seemed sincere. "Trust that we would not resort to such measures if things were not dire. We needed to enlist the help of the ghoul trader."

"Why's that? No one needs ghouls for anything."

"I assure you we certainly do. You see, the group responsible for the abduction of Pete—our most vital and treasured Keeper of the Story—is a cult of ghouls calling themselves The Church of the Lost."

Pearl explained how Pete had begged to join an expedition outside the Boomer's gates, insisting that this rare adventure outside their small, secluded world, was worthy of remembering in the Story, and that he should be there to see and remember it. Things had been fine until the group had been forced to take a different route home due to reports of super mutants patrolling the road they'd come up on. They detoured around a mountain, trying their best to stay hidden from Caesar's patrols and other dangers, when their campsite was ambushed in the middle of the night by a group of ghouls. They thought they were feral at first—the attack had been particularly vicious—but one of the survivors of the encounter was fully capable of speech, and rambled about "protecting and preserving the holy words of their prophet." When he started mentioning "the boy," it was then that they realized that Pete had been lost in the chaos of the attack, along with two other Boomers.

They tried to track and pursue the kidnappers, but it was difficult in the darkness, and they eventually came across large numbers of Legionary troops that the small, injured party couldn't hope to overcome. How the ghouls had managed to get through the dangers was a mystery to them. Before executing the captured ghoul attacker with an explosive they had taped across his chest, they found out that the Church of the Lost was located somewhere in the city of Los, on the other side of Caesar's territory.

"The city of Los is, apparently, a ghoul-only city," Pearl explained, "and they shoot any non-ghouls on sight. Even if we could cross Caesar's territory to get there, we have no way of getting to the church and finding Pete safely. A caravan crosses borders and enters cities without much suspicion, especially one led by a young, solitary ghoul trader."

"So you want me to go get him?"

"That's very perceptive. Yes, that is the favor we are asking of you, as a ghoul who is experienced in traveling the Wasteland."

Cooper chose not to correct her on that, and instead raised his metal-clad arm, "And what's this thing you've put on me?"

"A way of keeping track of you. It's a radio, among other things," she shrugged as if to say it was no big deal. "It will connect to a Mr. Gutsy unit we'll be providing you with for your journey, along with some other firepower. Believe me when I say you will not be going without ample equipment."

"Company and protection..." Cooper said, half to himself.

"Yes, to put it one way. There is one more request," Pearl stood up and disappeared briefly into a back room. She re-emerged holding a large steel contraption in both hands. It looked like a gun, but where there should have been a barrel, there was an open chamber with two rails on either side. Cooper guessed it was meant to launch something. He was right.

Pearl placed the device heavily on the table between them. "This is more of a personal request that I would like to kindly ask of you. You see, the Boomers have a policy: when facing an enemy, wipe them off the face of the Earth. This device here is an M-42 Tactical Nuclear Catapult, better known as the Fat Man. This one's been modified to shoot farther, and has a slot to load a backup round, in case you miss or just want to nuke something twice."

Cooper's eyes widened as he stared at the weapon. Like many born after the Great War, to Cooper the power of the atom was an almost mythical force of destruction. "You want me to take that with me?" he asked warily.

"Yes, and when you have brought Pete to safety, I want you to get somewhere high, point this thing at those bastards who thought to kidnap one of the Boomers' own, and erase them from history. Will you do this for us, my young ghoul friend?" Although smiling, her eyes—previously warm, apologetic, and motherly—had gone cold and hard as stone.

"Actually, I'm pretty busy, and have something I was on my way to do. This favor you're asking...Do I have a choice?" Cooper asked, staring at the iron cuff around his arm and knowing the answer.

"I suppose you really don't, no. I am sorry, as we are quite desperate. I promise you that you will come to no harm, so long as you carry out this task for us. I also promise you that we aren't asking you to do this for free, you understand. If there is anything you would have us do in return, name it, and we will try to accommodate you." Pearl spread out her hands in what Cooper supposed was a welcoming gesture.

Cooper laughed, a bit harshly, "You could buy all my caravan's stock at twice the rate and fly me home."

"Well, if it's trade you're after—"

"No, actually," Cooper cut her off, "I need to find a cure to a plague known as 116. It's destroying my settlement. Killing my father."

Cooper explained the mysterious illness which had driven him to take to the Wasteland in the first place in search of a cure. He talked about the possible hints that Dr. Tremain and Joshua Graham had given him towards those who might have an answer. He also emphasized how much he was running against the clock, not knowing when it might be too late to go back. Pearl listened intently, jotting down a few notes. She also sketched a few things on a map and handed it over to Cooper.

"This route should be the quickest way to Los. It will take you through Caesar's territory, so keep your head down, pay the tolls, and make haste, child. We will send out a party to inquire about 116. If you can bring back our Keeper safely, so that our story is not lost, we will do whatever we can to preserve that of North Fork."

She offered her hand to shake, and Cooper warily took it, starting again at the metal cuff that had been fastened to him. "You'd best hurry up, now," Pearl's grandmotherly smile was back as she released her grip, "The men have likely finished loading the caravan with your new supplies."

Cooper wasn't surprised they had been loading the caravan for him while Pearl spoke, considering he had never been in a position to turn down the mission outside of shooting his way out. He left the house and found the brahmin freshly watered and sporting a few extra packs. Good thing he had left North Fork with a light load. When he opened them, he found more weapons and ammunition, as well as the Fat Man launcher and two mini-nuke rounds. He covered them up with some cloth and a bundle of rope, not wanting to look at it. The Boomer soldier standing guard over the caravan also listed off some items that they could use in exchange for some scrap and electronics. Cooper charged them double.

When he and the brahmin had reached the gate, a Mr. Gutsy floated over to greet him. His body was painted in a black-and-blue color scheme to match with the jackets and coveralls of the Boomers. On his side was painted a rocket in colorful, cartoonish mid-explosion.

He spoke with a harsh, military tone that contrasted deeply with how polite he was. "Well met, sir. My name is Bockscar, and I will be assisting you on this mission in any way I can. How may I address you?"

"Cooper is fine," Cooper said into the non-blinking yellow eye.

"Aye aye, Master Cooper! Shall we move out?"

"Yes, but before that, one question." Cooper had been studying the contraption strapped to his arm ever since he noticed it, and from what he knew about mechanics, he was pretty sure he already knew the answer. "This is a bomb, isn't it?"

"Very good, sir! Well spotted! In the event that you forsake your mission, or if you are captured by the enemy, that will deliver a high-impact explosion, sir."

"And I suppose you won't let me try and take it off?"

"You can try, sir, but it is also rigged to explode if tampered with or damaged. I would not recommend it."

Cooper sighed. Now, along with arms dealers and spies, he could add 'walking bomb' to his list of qualifications. So much for a simple life trading goods on the road. He was still pretty buzzed from the tea, so he figured he might as well see how far the caravan could go into the night. The robot could keep watch. As they started walking, he turned to Bockscar.

"Bockscar, do you mind if I listen to the radio?"

"Not at all, Master Cooper! In fact, I am a mighty fine radio, myself, sir."

The music that came from somewhere in the robotic depths of the floating orb was clear and without static—perfect, really. Even still, Cooper thought that the voices had never sounded more hollow.

Dust whirls on the plain

Making patterns as we walk down lovers lane

Seems that each new step is somehow preordained

I've not traveled this way before

Green clouds in the sky

Seem forever but we know by-and-by

That they fade just like caravans passing by

Love seemed like that before

V. The Legion

A crimson flag waved gently in the morning sun against a cloudless blue sky, emblazoned with a golden bull that seemed restless in the wind, as if it were looking for someone to charge. Cooper had been unable to sleep, probably owing partly to his long drug-induced nap and the Boomers' special energy-boosting tea, so he and Bockscar had walked through the night. They needed to make up for lost time, after all. How many days had it been since he left North Fork? Nine? Ten? Too many, and it would be another three or four days to Los, assuming they didn't run into any...

"Halt! In the name of Caesar!"

"You've got to be kidding me," swore Cooper under

his breath.

The radio cut out, and he heard gears and mechanics sliding into place from his left as Bockscar readied his weapons, "Hostile targets acquired! Initiating—"

"No! No! Don't initiate anything!" hissed Cooper. "We're trying to get through here without trouble." Bockscar's weapons were still out, and his yellow eye had turned red. "Uh...stand down?" Cooper tried to remember military terminology he'd read about in his copies of *Astoundingly Awesome Tales*.

"Acknowledged, sir." Bockscar lowered his arms, his eye going back to yellow, but still firmly focused on the advancing Legionaries. Cooper could see them now, four soldiers in leather skirts and armor plating. Three were armed with spears topped with broad, gleaming blades and wore pistols at their sides. The fourth, leading the group in long strides towards the caravan, held a powerful hunting rifle similar to the one Two-Bears wielded. It probably wasn't full-auto, but Cooper wasn't eager to find out for sure or create a commotion, especially when there could be more Legionaries nearby. The leader raised his hand for a halt a few paces from where Cooper was standing. They held their weapons at the ready.

"What business do you have entering the territory of the Great Caesar?"

Cooper raised his hands in surrender, "I'm just here to trade. We're a small caravan trying to survive in the Wastes, sir."

"Why did you not take the normal roads? Were you attempting to sneak through the borders?" the head Legionary tightened his grip on his rifle.

Cooper stammered, partly for effect. "N-Not at all, no! I'm just, well, new you see. Taking over the caravan from my father and still learning about the big, wide world. Please, I-I just want to stop at a few towns, do my business, and keep going." Cooper wasn't sure if the sweat was from nerves or the increasing heat of the day as the sun climbed its way up. Probably both.

"Damn uncivilized dogs. Do you not have any respect for the rules of society?" The head Legionary paused a moment in thought and sighed. "Very well. We will escort you to the nearest town so that you may pay your toll and get on the proper roads. One suspicious move, and we will execute you on sight. Search his goods." With a look of annoyance, the leader waved his troops toward the caravan.

Cooper froze. If they saw the Fat Man, or any of the explosives the Boomers had given him, how would that look? The soldiers approached his brahmin and began poking through the bags and cases strapped to their sides. They didn't seem to be looking too thoroughly, so maybe the junk he'd piled on top of the mini-nukes would be enough for them to pass over. They got to the brahmin in the middle, Big Riz, who had taken on the cases from the Boomers. Cooper looked around for cover, but he was at the bottom of a hill, and the Legionaries would have higher ground over him immediately. If it came down to it, he'd have to make a run for it and hope that Bockscar could put those weapons to good use in his defense.

They opened the case where the mini-nukes were and Cooper held his breath. One of the Legionaries lifted some of the rope out and looked at it with a bored expression, letting it fall back in and closing the lid of the case. Cooper let out his breath and turned back to the leader, who was now leaning on his rifle and watching the Legionaries work.

"What are you guys doing out here, anyway?" Cooper ventured.

The leader looked at Cooper the way most people looked at a rotting bloatfly corpse in the road. He'd never read any comics about ghoul Legionaries, so Cooper wondered if this soldier had ever seen one—that wasn't feral, anyway. After making a dismissive noise, the leader continued in the same haughty tone he'd held since spotting the caravan.

"Not that it's any concern of yours, profligate, but

there have been reports of attacks on Legion patrols along the borders. We've also been on the lookout for weapons which we believe to have been stolen from honorable Legion soldiers who were ambushed."

"Stolen weapons?" Cooper asked, although his question was quickly answered by one of the Legionaries yelling, "Alexus! The .45s! There's a whole stock of them in here!"

All of a sudden, there was a machete pointed at him. So that's where Graham had liberated the weapons from. Cooper should have guessed there had been more to the easy job of bringing the guns with him. Then again, he probably hadn't thought that Cooper would go strolling into Caesar's territory with them in tow. Why hadn't he left them at the Boomers' base, anyway? A stupid, amateur mistake. He knew the Legion hated Joshua Graham and the New Canaanites, and here he had hauled a bunch of their signature weapons right across their borders. It was a mistake his father wouldn't have made. There was little time for regret, though, as the head Legionary was shouting and the machete looked very, very sharp.

"I shall repeat myself once more, slowly. Tell me where you got the guns, or I will turn you from a walking zombie into a proper corpse."

Playing innocent had worked before, so Cooper tried to lie again, laughing nervously.

"Okay, okay. I traded for them a few towns back. Heard the Legion would pay good money for them and was going to try and sell them here."

The leader sneered, "That seems unlikely, you rotting cur." He swung his machete to point towards the crate of .45s, now open. "The inside of that crate bears the mark of the Burned Man, traitor to Caesar and enemy of the Legion. You are no doubt an agent of his, and you shall die!"

Everything happened at once. Just as the Legionary went to turn back towards Cooper, his blade held above his head, glinting off the sun, an explosion hit just behind the man, taking one of his legs off at the knee and shredding the other one into a hopeless mess. The pressure from the explosion knocked into Cooper's chest and caused him to stumble backwards, his ears ringing. Over the din, he heard Bockscar's amplified voice, "Initiating defense protocols!"

Two of the Legionaries engaged with Bockscar—Cooper could hear small-arms fire ricocheting off his metal body—but one of them had broken off and was running over towards Cooper and the downed leader, who was bleeding onto the sand and trying to crawl towards his rifle. Cooper ran forward and kicked it away, ducking down just in time to hear a few shots from the advancing Legionary whiz by. He drew his .45 and leveled it, firing towards the exposed legs of the running Legionary. None of them found their mark, and he was almost on top of Cooper now. Thankful that the bullets had proven capable of going through Legionary armor, Cooper fired for the larger target that was the enemy's armored torso. They punched right through, and the Legionary cried out and fell forward mid-stride.

Cooper looked over to where Bockscar was fighting just in time to see a searing arc of flames engulf one of the Legionaries, who screamed and ran for a few steps before falling over. The remaining soldier wisely ran out of Bockscar's range, and looked to be heading up the hill, where he would probably try to call for help. Cooper grabbed the rifle he had kicked away from the head Legionary and looked down its sights, drawing in a deep breath and focusing, trying to slow things down. Either through luck, or his practice shooting flying pests, Cooper's first shot traveled straight and true directly through the non-helmeted skull of the escaping Legionary. He fell and rolled back down the hill, trailing blood behind him.

Cooper stood up, slinging the rifle over his back. He drew his .45 Auto again and reloaded it as he walked over to where the last Legionary—the leader, Alexus— was lying on the ground, his face contorted in pain and rage. Cooper finished reloading and looked at the gun, remembering a time when his father had been preparing to leave for The Rounds, checking and loading up a pistol. In his memory, he heard that conversation from years ago.

"Dad, have you ever killed anyone with that gun? Like, people?"

His father had set the gun down and paused, turning around and coming over to kneel down in front of Cooper. He put his hands on Cooper's shoulders.

"When I'm out there in the Wastes, I've always done everything I can to avoid having to fight other people, but..." a sad look passed over his face, settling into a frown across his scarred, cracked lips, "There are some people out there who want to hurt others so they can get what they want, or who think you're an enemy and attack because the world out there has made them violent and scared. I always do my best to talk, bargain, lie, anything I need to do to keep from using that gun on anything other than radscorpions and night stalkers, but sometimes you have

no choice. Sometimes, I had no choice."

"So you really have?" Cooper had asked quietly.

"Yes. Yes, I have, Cooper. Because whenever I was out there, the picture I kept in my head was of this room, of you and all the people in North Fork that were depending on me to come back alive. It wasn't easy, and it never gets easier, but if you go out there and it's you or the other guy with you in his sights, you do whatever you can to come back and protect your own. You fight to make it home."

Back in the desert, standing far enough away that the crippled Legionary couldn't strike him with the machete he still gripped tightly in his hand, Cooper leveled the .45 Auto at the man's head.

"Curse you, Canaanite dog!" the man spat.

Cooper could have left him there. He wasn't a threat anymore. But something had gotten his blood up, and suddenly his heart was pounding with excitement rather than fear. He looked the Legionary in the eyes and smiled, "Those guns? I did get them from Joshua

Graham. He told me to give you this." He pulled the trigger, and the Legionary's head became a spray of red gore across the sand.

Cooper closed his eyes, drew in a deep breath, and searched the man's body, finding a detailed map of Legion territory, along with ammo and currency. He checked the other bodies before whistling for the caravan to continue. Bockscar floated over to him, "Nice shooting, sir! What an act of bravery and valor!"

Cooper didn't reply, but just walked up the ridge towards the waypoint his looted map indicated would keep him on the path towards Los. When they reached the top, he looked back over the carnage. He saw some radroaches were already crawling out of the cracks between the rocks to scavenge on the corpses. It was likely the bodies would be gone before long, disappeared as if they'd never been there. He reached into his pocket and felt the medallion that Two-Bears had taken from Cooper's first kill. His father had been right, the Wasteland belonged to the killers, but he had been wrong about one thing:

It did get easier.

He reached First Mesa, the nearest Legion settlement, later that day, and the guards outside the fence gave him no trouble when he said he was there to trade on behalf of the ghoul settlement of North Fork. His father had said that, thanks to their resistance to rads, the sort of scrap they were able to get was generally considered as rare and worth taking a look at. That reputation had let a single caravan keep a settlement like North Fork from dying out. Cooper entered the small grouping of makeshift buildings that made up the settlement, and found a place to rest the brahmin and set up.

Cooper figured he could spend the rest of the day conducting trades, maybe even staying in First Mesa for the night. The settlers didn't have much in the way of mechanical parts or any currency, but they did have a surprisingly large amount of chems, which they scavenged and supplied to the Legion. Ghouls didn't eat or drink as much as a non-mutated human, but chems that caused addiction or psychosis in humans worked like medicine for them. Cooper reckoned Doctor Tremain would be happy as he managed to trade for a good stock of Jet, Buffout, Turbo, and something he'd never seen before that the seller called "Hydra," which he claimed could restore crippled limbs.

Ghouls also enjoyed a good, strong drink. "Stuff that'll kill a smoothskin outright," one of the older residents of North Fork, a squat man named Arnie, had said while laughing in a voice that was weighed down by booze. Although Cooper didn't have much in the way of drinking experience, he knew that the selection of homemade Legion rot-gut and potent-looking brews sloshing around in bottles of various colors and sizes would be welcome at the next party held in North Fork.

Assuming there was anyone left to celebrate when Cooper got back. Assuming he could find a cure. Arnie wouldn't be there, at the very least. He was the first taken by 116.

These dark thoughts were interrupted by a hearty "*Ave, young trader!*" Cooper looked over to see a tall, thin man in red and gold armor, flanked on either side by large Legionary guards, carrying an ornate, crested helmet under his arm.

"I see that it is true," he continued as he walked over, "There is indeed a ghoul caravan in town. How fortuitous that my patrol has brought us to this backwater settlement. Pray, tell me, do you know the name Thomas Pulman?"

Cooper was taken aback. He decided to tell the truth, "Yes. He's my father."

"Your father? I see. How very interesting this is. You will stay the night." It wasn't a question. "Come with me, and tell me how you came to be here." One of the guards had moved to Cooper's side and laid a hand on his shoulder to guide him forward.

Once inside, the man introduced himself as Aurelius of Phoenix. The Grognak comics, beers, and cigarettes inside his room and makeshift office didn't seem to match his stern-looking face, nor did his persistent smile match the implied threat of the ever-present guards blocking the door. Cooper wasn't sure what to make of him, but since he hadn't killed him on sight, guessed that no word of his encounter with the Legionaries or his father's history with Joshua Graham had reached him. Cooper told him his story so far, carefully sidestepping around his newer cargo. Aurelius listened with intent interest, and expressed his sympathies when Cooper finished.

"Like many, I knew and liked your father," he said.

"I'm learning he's very popular," Cooper replied.

"Indeed. Did you know he did business with the Legion? It's true. Carried out a few tasks for us. Very good at Caravan, if I recall. Do you play, Cooper?"

Aurelius made a motion at one of the guards, who went to a nearby table and picked up two packs of cards.

"It's been a while, but, yes. My father taught me," Cooper said with some suspicion.

"Oh, then this should be *very* interesting. You see, I could never beat Thomas in a game of Caravan."

"You played *cards* with my father?" Cooper tried to picture it.

"You look surprised. Did you think that a Centurion in Caesar's Legion would not enjoy a game of cards? Life in the Legion may be strict, boy, but it is not without its divertissements, especially out here on the borders."

Aurelius laid the two decks on the table between them. "So, what do you say we play a hand? And, of course, what would a game of Caravan be without something at stake?" He smiled, and something dangerous glinted in his hard, blue eyes, "Let's say that, should you win, we will escort you to any destination within Caesar's borders, at double the speed you can move on your own. Our chariots are quite fast, you see, and capable of moving your brahmin and all your goods."

"I'm almost afraid to ask this, but what if I lose?" asked Cooper.

The smile on Aurelius's face stayed, but hardened, and his voice grew cold, with a razor-sharp edge. "Then I confiscate those weapons you're carrying for the Burned Man, as well as the rest of your cargo, and send you off into the night to fend for yourself." Cooper went to stand up, but heavy hands from the guards behind him forced him back into his seat.

Aurelius continued, his voice staying at the same low, dangerous tone. "You thought your goods would not be checked? Or that you could wear one of my scouts' rifles on your back and not raise any attention? I assume your father taught you better than that."

Cooper struggled against the guards' grip, hoping to maybe grab a weapon.

"Now, no reason to escalate things into conflict. Like I said, life here is strict, but it does not have to be lethally so. Entertain me, and everything will turn out fine for you. Take a deck, and let us play."

The guards released him. Cooper didn't see much of an alternative. He thought about telling Aurelius about the bomb, and using it to bluff his way out of there. Or maybe trying to signal Bockscar, whom he had left to watch the caravan. Deliberating, he looked at the table where the decks of cards were, and saw for the first time the piles of NCR dog tags there and elsewhere along the room. They told Cooper three things: Auerlius liked his trophies, he was not to be lightly crossed, and he was probably not easily intimidated. He decided to play, and try and shoot his way out if he lost.

"Alright, I'll play," said Cooper, "but I'd like to use my own deck." Slowly, under the guards watch, he reached inside one of the coat's many pockets and found what he was looking for: his father's Caravan deck. When he put it on the table, he thought he saw Aurelius's eyes widen slightly, and then he laughed. Cooper allowed himself to smile a little and drew his starting cards.

As they played, Aurelius asked him where he was intending to go. Cooper explained about the Church of the Lost, and the city of ghouls just outside the Legion's borders. He left out the part about having a powerful explosive strapped to his arm, just in case he needed to use it for bargaining his way out later, and also because it would ruin the mood of the game.

"So you are doing this as a service to the Boomers. I see. How very like your father. Along his trading routes, he often picked up odd jobs and offered his unique set of skills." Aurelius was getting close to finishing up one of his caravans, and Cooper wasn't drawing what he needed for his own in order to outbid his opponent.

"You mentioned he did some work for you in the past," Cooper said as casually as he could manage.

"Yes. In fact, the Legion tried to recruit him to work

exclusively for us as one of the Frumentarii."

"A ghoul in the Legion?" Cooper was genuinely surprised at this, as his father had never had any kind words to say about the Legion's actions.

"Why not? We accepted Gaius Magnus and his crimson guard after the incident at Dry Wells. The Legion cares only for the strength and skill of its men, not how much skin they have on their face." Aurelius tapped his nose, then discarded and drew a new card, his smile widening as he looked at it.

"But my father didn't join you?" Cooper asked, deciding to disband the caravan opposite Aurelius's nearly completed one, hoping for a better draw in time to salvage the game.

"No. Ironically, he claimed that ghouls were 'too old for cults of personality.' I suppose if you do make it to Los, you will see about proving him wrong." Aurelius finished one of the caravans at 25. "Although that's looking less likely," Aurelius said confidently. Cooper would need to rebuild the caravan he had just disbanded to a perfect 26, or otherwise rely on the other two to beat his bids.

"What do you know about the city of Los?" Cooper asked, trying to keep his focus on the game as he listened.

"We do not interfere or interact with them much. It would seem that Caesar has little interest in conquering them, as of yet. However, I have heard rumors that they are seeking a way to bring about another Great War. They would not be the first, and I doubt they will be successful. But do not underestimate the power of a 'cult of personality' which your father scoffed at, Cooper."

"Why's that?" asked Cooper.

"Devotion, dedication, honor, purpose, drive, these are all very powerful tools for motivating man and ghoul alike. These are things that followers of a strong leader will not hesitate to kill or die for. If you intend to disrupt the Church of the Lost, you will not find it easy."

Aurelius discarded, drew a new card, and began to laugh. "And you may find it nearly impossible after losing this game." He played his card, it was a Joker, played on an Ace of Diamonds, meaning that all diamonds on the table would be removed. Aurelius barely had any, but the larger numbers in Cooper's caravans were all diamonds. Aurelius sat back, looking victorious.

Cooper had been doing his best to keep a straight face, but now it was his turn to laugh. This was absolutely perfect!

"What are you laughing at with those pathetic cards of yours?" Aurelius looked genuinely confused.

"My father's deck has no pathetic cards," Cooper said, playing his first card, a King of Hearts from the Lux Casino. "I feel like I should thank you. My caravans were all stuck at bids just under yours, and I couldn't seem to get the cards to bump them up. But now that you've reset them a little," he played another King, "I can use all these Kings I was holding onto. Really lucky my father traveled so much," Cooper played another King. "Because, I have to tell you, this deck is just loaded with Kings. I didn't get how to use them, at first, but it's about doubling and working with what you already have on the table, not rushing to stock up ahead of your opponent." Cooper played his last one and sat back himself. "Well, looks like the game's over."

On Cooper's side of the table were three caravans all worth 26 points. By sheer luck, or perhaps the design of his father's deck, he was able to attach all of his Kings to cards that doubled in value perfectly.

"I...I can't believe it." Aurelius said, staring at the table. His hand flashed out, and Cooper reached for his weapon. The guards brought their spears to either side of Cooper's neck, and things were gravely still until Cooper looked down and realized that Aurelius was extending his open hand. Cooper took his hand off his gun and reached out, and Aurelius shook it vigorously. The spears retracted from their uncomfortably close positions, and Cooper blinked in disbelief.

"That was very well played!" exalted Aurelius. "A much better game than I've gotten out of anyone in a long time. I forgot about those damned Kings that Thomas kept in his deck," the Centurion shook his head and chuckled. "Well, I am a man of my word. We will see you off in the morning, and I will ask no further questions about the weapons you are smuggling," he stopped shaking Cooper's hand and suddenly pulled him closer, "Other Legionaries you run into will not be as generous or understanding. If they find those, you may wind up decorating one of the crosses along the Great Road."

With that ominous warning, Aurelius saw Cooper out of his room, and instructed the guards to arrange a place for him to stay. It did not escape his notice that there was a guard posted outside his door as he settled in for bed, but it was still nice not to be sleeping on the ground for once, or to be sleeping six feet under it, for that matter.

He had been told that they would leave at first light, which was probably in a few short hours. Whatever these "chariots" were, it would still take them almost two days to reach the outer border near Los. Despite his need for sleep, his head was full of questions and the looming mystery of Los. Not for the first time, he thought about the things his father had done out here in the Wasteland, and kicked himself for not having asked for more than entertaining stories of adventure. Cooper wasn't sure his father would have told him everything, anyway, but he hoped that they would have a chance on his return to North Fork.

I-40 was the main artery through which the lifeblood of Caesar's Legion flowed—supplies, weapons, slaves, and anything else needed to keep the ever-expanding empire alive. After losing their battle for control of New Vegas, the Legion had turned its attention to the unclaimed east, and it was towards the east that Cooper was now headed. The sun was setting behind them, and they had already been traveling for two full days along the straight, seemingly endless line of the road carved into the desert, passing through towns showing various signs of life and reconstruction. The vast amount of Caesar's territory was incredible when actually traveled, and seeing the flags and Legionaries in town after town both impressed and frightened Cooper.

The man leading the escort, Pecus Domitor, assured Cooper they'd reach the border by nightfall, which meant that Cooper was nearly at the end of this rescue mission he'd been forced into. For the thousandth time since his run-in with the Boomers, Cooper fiddled carefully with the metal cuff around his forearm.

He had been woken up the morning after his high-stakes game of Caravan by the sounds of cargo being loaded and loud animal cries. The animals turned out to be something the soldiers in First Mesa called "asinii," and looked like less noble versions of the animals carved into the heads of the Dead Horses war clubs. They hooked a team of them to fenced-in wheeled platforms, which Aurelius informed Cooper were used for quickly transporting livestock and slaves along I-40. The beasts moved much faster than Cooper would have imagined just by looking at their gray, lackluster appearance, and they certainly moved faster than the caravan of brahmin did even when they were in a good mood.

When he expressed this, Pecus proudly explained that, ever since finding a herd of the beasts during a raid to conquer nearby settlements, and bringing them into the Legion, they had been experimenting with different cross-breeding techniques to improve their supply lines between the ever-growing empire of Caesar. Cooper got along well with Pecus, and the two passed their time talking about caravan animals, dangers along trade routes, and other various minutiae of the job. Cooper found himself genuinely interested in the conversation, and then struck by the absurdity of talking shop with his somewhat benevolent captors while riding through Legion territory on a contraption pulled by animals he had never seen before, all while traveling to assassinate the leader of a ghoul cult in a town he had never heard of because he had a bomb strapped to him by a group of heavily armed settlers looking for a favor.

He fell into a fit of laughter, the gasping, uncontrollable sort, and was unable to explain it to Pecus, waving him off and leaving him to wonder about the strange young ghoul he'd been charged with taking to the border.

When Cooper finally finished, he took a deep breath and said only, "I've just been learning a lot about life in the Wasteland this past week or two."

"*Usus magister est optimus*," replied Pecus, "Experience is the best teacher. You spend enough time out here, it changes you. You either learn and grow, or you die."

They reached a small outpost and toll station along the road after nightfall. Lit by flickering orange torchlight in the middle of the blackness, it was manned by two bored-looking Legionaries who were assigned to look out for caravans or travelers and impose the fee for using Caesar's road, which was patrolled and generally free of Raiders. Pecus explained the situation to the guards, and they began to unload the brahmin off the chariots.

He walked over to Cooper, "This is our outer border. Los should be another day or two of travel to the southeast, depending on your pace. You can camp here, if you wish, but I must return to my duties. The wheels of the Legion are always turning, and, like you, I have deliveries to make."

"Thank you, Pecus. This trip has definitely been enlightening."

"May we meet again on the road, Cooper. Perhaps someday Zion Canyon will join the Legion, and your caravan can work for the mighty Caesar."

The thought unsettled Cooper, but he appreciated the sentiment, regardless, so he simply said his farewells and got the brahmin moving again. They seemed as ready to be on the move as Cooper was after days of cramped riding. As they went to pass the border checkpoint, one of the Legionaries waved him over.

"*Ave*, trader. A word, if you will."

"What is it?" asked Cooper.

"Posted out here, we hear reports from the caravans and travelers that come from the uncivilized eastern wilderness. Pecus said that you were heading towards Los, but I wouldn't recommend it."

"Why? What have you heard about Los?"

"It used to be a big trading stop, but the city has closed itself to normal humans, and is enshrouded in some kind of dense, poisonous fog. People passing through disappear into it and are never seen again, and there's talk of some kind of a civil war, a secret cult, and maybe even Brotherhood soldiers. Even for a ghoul, I don't think it's safe."

"It's probably not," Cooper agreed, "but I don't have much of a choice." Cooper lowered his voice to a conspiratorial whisper, "I'm a ticking time-bomb, you see." The Legion soldier looked confused and worried, so Cooper laughed. "Ghoul humor, sorry. There's something I need to do in Los. Thank you for the warning, anyway."

"If you're going to go, at least stay off the main road. If those brahmin can handle rocky terrain, I would go south until you hit the river, then follow it until you see an old bridge and a cluster of abandoned buildings along the water."

"How do you know all this?" asked Cooper.

"I wasn't always in the Legion, kid, like a lot of people. I got tired of fighting every day just to survive out there. The Legion took me in and they protected their people against the savagery out there," he gestured into the darkness. "Turns people into monsters. Take care of yourself."

Cooper nodded and whistled for the caravan to move out into the darkness. The outpost had at least let him take a torch, and he could only hope it kept away anything that was also awake out there. With sleep a far off prospect, and a full night of walking ahead of him, Cooper decided to turn the radio on low, hoping that the familiarity of the tinny sound would help settle his busy, wearied mind.

Yes, I've got heartaches by the number

A love that I can't win

But the day that I stop counting

That's the day my world will end

Heartache number three was when you called me

And said that you were coming back to stay

With hopeful heart I waited for your knock on the door

I waited but you must have lost your way

VI. The Lost

Before he ever saw the Bridge of Los, Cooper knew he was going the right direction. He had walked throughout the night and the following day, stopping only for short breaks, and at first he thought the signs were hallucinations brought on by exhaustion or the Turbo he'd taken from his traded stock after drinking some extra Boomer tea. Each of the signs stood like a monolith in the middle of the rocks and sand, and each was painted in red with an upside down star and messages like: PURGE MAN RISE GHOULS and GHOULS ARE THE NEW WORLD. After the third or fourth one he came across, Cooper realized they were marking a path straight towards Los, and that maybe his approach wasn't going to be as discreet as he had hoped.

That night, he reached the bridge the border guard had told him about. At its entrance was a large wooden board, scrawled in the same red as the ominous signposts had been. This one said: THOSE WHO WERE LOST WILL INHERIT THE EARTH FROM THE FAILED AGE OF MAN. Hanging from a makeshift gallows next to the sign were several figures, long dead and some with limbs missing, either scavenged or removed prior to their execution. Cooper assumed that none of the bodies would be ghoul ones. Backlit by the lights of a warehouse complex on the opposite shore of the river, Cooper could see them twist and swing, stirred by a warm breeze that made him shiver all the same.

"Bockscar?" he spoke up. The robot had been floating silently since their encounter with the Legion. His presence had made them nervous, and Cooper had to negotiate just to allow him to be brought with them on the chariots.

"Yes, sir?" Bockscar replied.

"If things get...bad in there. Can you help out?"

"That is my mission, sir."

"And if I get captured? Or killed?"

"You will explode, sir."

"And what about you?"

"I will go home and report on your explosion."

"I see. Thanks," Cooper said dryly.

"You're most welcome, sir."

Cooper hoped the robot would give him a little time before triggering the bomb if he got captured, but had no way of knowing for sure, so he shrugged and pushed on. Things had been working out so far, so maybe he'd be alright.

Standing just a few feet along the bridge were two armed guards. They weren't talking. They weren't moving or fidgeting or smoking or anything—just looking into the distance like statues. Cooper didn't see much choice but to approach. For the first time since leaving North Fork, he decided to put the hood of his coat down, his scarred and deformed features in full view, hoping that it might grant him some clemency.

Before he moved forward, he checked and reloaded his pistols and rifle, and checked the crate where the Fat Man lay in wait. He nodded at it, gave Pook a pat on his heads, and moved the caravan towards the bridge and the city of Los beyond it.

He was nearly on top of the two guards before they finally spoke, in unison, "The Church of the Lost and its prophet Blake the Seeker welcomes its ghoul brethren who cry out in this land and seek to escape the tyranny of man. Join us, and find peace. Join us, and preserve our future. Join us, and create a new home for our people."

"Um...hi there," replied Cooper.

Thankfully, only one spoke this time, "Do you approach the Bridge of Truth in order to seek counsel and solace from the Prophet Blake?" He stared directly into Cooper's eyes with a single eye. The other was missing somewhere in the half of his face that was a melting ruin of flesh. Cooper found it hard to lie under that gaze, but he did anyway.

"Yes?" he said in a mix of statement and question, then quickly added, "and to trade goods and supplies."

There was a long pause while Cooper and the one-eyed guard locked their three eyes, then the other guard spoke up, causing Cooper to jump a little.

"Where have you come from, Child of the Lost?" This second guard was missing the opposite eye, and for a crazy moment Cooper had to stifle laughter while he wondered if the powers that be had planned things like that, combing their cult ranks for two symmetrically disfigured members. The second guard was also much bigger, however, and held a spiked hammer effortlessly over his shoulders, so Cooper didn't feel like laughing for very long.

"A long way away. I was fleeing Caesar's Legion and their, uh...tyranny." Cooper wasn't very good at this undercover spy thing, he was finding. It seemed to work anyway, because the two guards stood aside and silently motioned over the bridge. Cooper whistled for the caravan to move. Just as he was passing between the two of them, they again spoke out in unison. "The Red Star will be your guide to the Home of the Lost. May Blake welcome you with open arms into a new Brotherhood of Superior Life."

"Um, thanks, brothers," said Cooper as he kept walking.

The bridge was a wide concrete structure, and along its sides were more of those wooden signs, which now bore such messages as WELCOME HOME, NO LONGER LOST, BLAKE IS THE LIGHT, and other warm, loving phrases posted above the occasional human body sprawled along the bridge. It looked like there had once been a row of market stalls or something along here, before every man, woman, and child with smooth skin was massacred and left to lay where they died. After a while, he just kept his view straight ahead until he reached the end of the bridge. Looking to his right, he saw the main warehouse, its doors wide open and light pouring out into the night. Above the door was the upside-down red star. Again there were two guards posted, and again they were completely still until Cooper had hesitantly walked through the doors, which prompted them to say "Welcome, brother" in matching machine-like voices. They then closed the doors in a synchronized motion, leaving Bockscar and the brahmin outside.

"I'm afraid that any non-ghoul companions are not allowed to enter the Church of the Lost," a hunched figure in a dirty purple robe was walking towards him in halting steps. He stopped in front of Cooper and straightened a little, pulling back his hood to reveal patches of white, wiry hair on his burned and blackened skull. He was also missing an eye, which Cooper was beginning to suspect wasn't a coincidence here in the Church of the Lost.

"Are you Blake?" Cooper asked.

"This humble form could not hope to measure up to the majestic greatness that is the Prophet. No, I am Bertrand, merely one of Blake's disciples, here to welcome newly arrived refugees from the world of man."

"Is it possible to see him? I'm, uh, interested in his message. About ghouls," Cooper clarified needlessly.

"Of course," Bertrand smiled, "The Prophet Blake is happy to personally receive those who wish to listen to his words of salvation and truth. I believe he is currently at work in his study. I will take you to him, but you will, of course, have to leave your weapons here with Reiss."

Cooper was suddenly aware of someone standing just behind him, waiting patiently. How was it that guards were constantly sneaking up and standing behind him? Was his perception really so low? He reminded himself to start keeping his back to a wall as he took the .45 Auto out of its holster and the rifle off his back and handed them over to Reiss, who had the same stiff posture and statue-like stillness, and whose single remaining eye was murky red around the edges. Cooper waited to see if they would pat him down or anything, but Reiss merely nodded, turned, and disappeared through a nearby door. Cooper made a note of where it was, but wasn't left completely unarmed. He could feel the weight of his father's 10mm still in one of his coat pockets.

"Right this way," Bertrand gestured. He led Cooper down a tight, dark hallway. Some of the doors they passed were open, and Cooper could see that many of the ghouls (all robed in the same dirty purple) were hunched over and writing with focus and speed.

"What are they working on?" Cooper asked.

"It is our great work, given to us by the Prophet. It is our testament and record to what is created here, so that all may share in the new life Blake is creating."

Bertrand spoke with quiet reverence, with pride quivering on its edges.

"Why did you join up with all this?"

"Have you not experienced the hardships that face our kind out there?" Bertrand returned. "Many of us are lost, hiding ourselves in dark corners or underground, living on and on and to what purpose? To wait until we lose our minds and become the monsters *they* believe us to be?" Bertrand had stopped, "Or to be something greater?" He jabbed his finger into Cooper's chest to punctuate his point. "Blake believes that we can be more. And I believe in him. You will see."

They continued walking, and the hallway soon opened up into an enormous chamber. Cooper guessed it had once been a factory floor of some kind, but now it was lit with hundreds of candles along the walls and scaffolding. There were makeshift pews made of scrap wood and metal, as well as an elaborate altar raised above the floor, sitting behind a flat table that, even though it was decorated with mosaic patterns made of colored broken glass, seemed more clinical than religious.

"Excuse me a moment while I confer with Blake about your arrival," Bertrand gave a slight bow then disappeared behind a small door to the side of the main altar. Cooper decided to take the opportunity to investigate his surroundings, in the highly likely event that he needed to make a quick exit. During their walk, he had been looking inside rooms and down hallways for Pete. Hoping for any hint at where the church might be keeping a human child whose primary talents were remembering and recording history.

Realization came to Cooper suddenly in a quick, cold spread. All the robed ghouls diligently scribbling away in their rooms. Talk of a new great work. He was pretty sure he knew where he would find Pete, and he was pretty sure he was alive—for now, at least. Chances are Blake had something specific he needed Pete for beyond a simple hostage or ransom, and that would mean he'd be unwilling to let Cooper just walk out here with him. He looked at the iron cuff and wondered how much monitoring the Boomers could do through it. Could they hear his conversations? Even with Bockscar outside, would they know what was happening here and, if Cooper failed, would they detonate the device immediately? Was the little red light on it blinking faster than it had been before, or was Cooper just imagining it? Well, he hoped his hunch about Blake and Pete was right, and he hoped that he'd be able to figure something out before he ran out of time.

As he was looking around the room, Cooper heard the door open again, and Bertrand called for him to enter. He touched his coat pocket where the pistol was, stiffened his shoulders, and walked in.

Blake's study was a dark, cramped room piled high with books and paper, and also looked like it was used as his bedroom and laboratory, with a cot off in the corner and several workbenches piled high with still more books, glass containers, and various small tools.

It was lit both by candles and a single artificial light over the workbench, which flickered on and off at random times, making the shadows leap and shudder nervously. Blake himself was currently pacing in the middle of the room, his purple hooded cape trailing behind him as he turned about. He cut an impressive, intimidating figure, standing at least 7 feet tall and covered in muscles underneath his scarred flesh, reminding Cooper less of a ghoul and more of a super mutant caravan guard he and his father had met in the canyon while traveling between the tribes. Although Blake looked decidedly less friendly, he certainly talked a hell of a lot more.

"If the doors of perception were cleansed everything would appear to man as it is, infinite."

"….excuse me?" said Cooper.

"What is grand is necessarily obscure to weak men. That which can be made explicit to the idiot is not worth my care," continued Blake, seemingly unaware.

"The Prophet is speaking his Truth so that it may be recorded," Bertrand explained from Cooper's side.

"Who's recording it?" Cooper asked, and Bertrand gestured to the back corner, where a young boy sat behind a small desk covered in stacks of carefully arranged paper. He was dirty and tired-looking, but otherwise unharmed—both his eyes were where they should be, at least. They were dark eyes that darted back and forth, focusing intently on the page in front of him as he wrote, his hair hanging in his face. Cooper almost called out to him, but remembered his cover and decided to stay silent for the moment.

"As a man is, so he sees. As the eye is formed, such are its powers." Blake paused after this last one, and finally turned to look at Cooper. Most of his face was obscured by his low hood, save for his mouth, which was grinning and full of teeth. "Who is it that comes to speak with me?" Blake asked, as Bertrand bowed out of the room.

"Um, my name is Cooper. I'm a ghoul from North

Fork, on the other side of Caesar's territory."

"Greetings, Cooper from North Fork, and welcome to my sanctuary," Blake spread open his large hands. "Have you come to listen to my wisdom? Or do you seek something?"

"Well, I'm just a caravan merchant, but," Cooper figured it couldn't hurt to ask about the plague. "My father and family—all ghouls, of course—are suffering from a plague called 116. Do you know anything about it?"

"Ah, 116. Yes, it is a creation of the human military to target those of our people they have deemed to be 'feral' or just 'dangerous.' Make no mistake, it is a means by which to extinguish our race. Yet, *great things are done when men and mountains meet,* and *the true method of knowledge is experiment.*"

"Experiments?" Cooper asked.

"Have faith, my brother. All things are going in accordance with the Plan. *This world's fiction is made up of contradictions.*" His dramatic preaching voice had returned and he looked back to the boy in the corner, "Did you record that, boy?"

The boy nodded, his eyes never leaving the paper, and Cooper noticed for the first time the chains piled around his feet. Cooper's eyes widened, and he quickly returned his attention to Blake.

"What's all the writing?" he asked him.

"*I must create a system or be enslaved by another mans; I will not reason and compare: my business is to create.*" Blake looked into the candles, "I became as I am only 30 years ago, mere minutes compared to some of our race. And yet, even in such a short time, I have experienced the shame of the place given to us by the smooth skinned men of the outside. All ghouls were forced, through man's folly, into this fate." Blake's voice began to speed up, and he growled with building anger, "I have also learned that we, however, are superior to them. *Make your own rules or be a slave to another man's.* Where this poisoned world is deadly to them, it strengthens us. This new world is *our* world. For too long we have been rotting away in the background, scattered and afraid, but soon we will rise up and spread across this land to reclaim the world from their undeserving hands. By blood and fire if we must. *The Deathclaws of wrath are wiser than the brahmin of instruction.*"

"That didn't answer my question, but okay." Cooper said. Blake heedlessly continued on.

"The writings—my wisdom and our ways recorded and preserved for the ages—are but one part of the Plan. The Prophet's Book shall be used to educate our new converts as we grow in number. *What is now proved was once only imagined.*" Another large, toothy grin from Blake. Cooper was actually somewhat relieved that he couldn't see his eyes (or eye), as he imagined the look in them would be less than sane. Blake went back to pacing like a caged animal.

"We shall become something greater than human. Something divine. *Cruelty has a human heart, And*

Jealousy a human face; Terror the human form divine, And Secrecy the human dress. The dress of ghoul is forged iron, the form of ghoul a fiery forge, the face of ghoul a furnace sealed, the heart of ghoul it's hungry gorge."

Cooper could barely follow the thread of his ramblings, and wondered what his chances would be in the small room if he just tried to shoot him now while he was absorbed in his prophesying and poetry. He didn't get the chance though, because just as Cooper slid his hand inside his coat pocket, the walls were shaken by the low boom of an explosion outside. After a few seconds, Bertrand burst back into the room.

"There is an attack outside! The guards are already on their way to protect you, my Prophet."

"There is no need. *When a sinister person means to be your enemy, they always start by trying to become your friend.*" Blake reached between two of the workbenches and removed a spear that was longer than Cooper was tall, with a full-size blade attached to the end of it. He spun and strode towards Cooper, who started to pull out his pistol, but Blake quickly grabbed his other wrist, dragging him over to the wall and locking him into a metal cuff there.

Blake brought his face close to Cooper's, talking through his teeth, "I will investigate this attack, and see what fruit this tree bears, and whether it gives way to truth, or wrath. Lock the door," Blake said to Bertrand, then ran out of the room. Bertrand narrowed his eyes at Cooper before he left, and Cooper heard a lock slide shut. He took a moment to catch his breath. His arm was throbbing in pain where Blake had grabbed it in a vice-like grip—he was inhumanly strong. Cooper would have to be sure to stay far away from him and that bladed spear if he ran into Blake again. First things first, he called out to the boy.

"Pete? Are you Pete?"

The boy was silent, but had stopped writing.

"Pete, I know I'm not doing a great job so far, but Pearl

sent me to rescue you. It's going to go a lot better from now on. I promise."

"You don't know the things he does..." Pete said in a quiet voice. "He's...taking people and...changing them."

"What?" Cooper shook his head. "That doesn't matter right now. Hold on a second." He rummaged with his free hand into his coat until he found what he was looking for: a set of lock-picking tools. His father had told him that all the best scrap and all the safest places to stay were behind locks, and that nobody locked up anything they didn't care about losing. Thankfully, Blake had only cuffed one of Cooper's hands in his rush, and the cuff itself was simple. Cooper had it off in a few seconds, and ran over to work on Pete's chains.

"If he catches us..." Pete started.

"I'll kill him," Cooper finished. "Or something. Look, I've got a lot on the line here." Pete looked scared, so Cooper winked at him to try and lighten the mood, but from Pete's confused reaction, it didn't seem to work—probably because the eye he winked with didn't have a full lid to cover it. "Never mind. Let's go." He unlocked the chains and pulled them off Pete's ankles, which were bruised and scratched in a few places.

"Can you walk?" he asked and Pete nodded. Cooper ran over to work on the door, which must have locked from the outside to prevent Pete, or whomever else Blake trapped in here over the years, from escaping. It was no more complicated than the other locks, though, and Cooper heard the satisfying click of the pins moving out of the way. "Stay behind me," he said to Pete and brought out his pistol, opening the door as he did so. Bertrand must have run off with Blake, because Cooper didn't see him outside. He started to move towards the exit when Pete called out to him from the desk he was still sitting at.

"The people Blake took," he said, "They take them somewhere over there. We have to help them. Two of them are my friends. Boomers."

Cooper thought it over for a second, and decided that it was probably best to try and find another exit that wasn't the front door anyway. "Will you still come with me if I say no?" he asked the boy. Pete shook his head solemnly. "Well, alright then. Easy decision, I guess. You damn Boomers don't really do the whole negotiating or polite request thing, do you?"

Cooper filled Pete in on his run-in with the Boomers as they went down the hallway Pete indicated. Pete was inquisitive, not only about Cooper's journey thus far, but about ghouls in general, which he'd never met before. Cooper told him what he could, keeping his voice low, and couldn't help but feel he was being studied like a subject in a museum.

The lights weren't kept on in this part of the compound, so it was dark except for the flickering light coming from the main chamber. Cooper crouched down a bit to try and move stealthily, a skill he wasn't really familiar with.

"It must be one of these doors ahead," Pete said, also

crouching. His voice, which had grown more mature since his release, sounded briefly again like a scared child, "At night, I hear...screaming from this direction sometimes. And music."

He checked a few of the doors as he crept down the hall: storage closet, toilet, storage closet, lockers. He pocketed a few useful-looking things, but saw no sign of prisoners. They had rounded a corner and gone through another set of doors when they heard it: a scream of agony barely audible under the sounds of a radio set to a pretty, carefree song and turned to full volume.

Let's go native

Sun your cares away

Be creative

Learn to live and play

Pretty flowers need the sun

This applies to everyone

Life's worth living

When nature's giving

Happiness to everyone

So let's go sunning

VII. The Truth

Quietly, Cooper approached and opened the door, pistol at the ready. He was looking into a small office lit only by the greenish glow of a computer terminal. A ghoul in a medical coat was sitting behind a desk surrounded by filing cabinets and busily typing away, the monitor's light reflecting off of his reading glasses, which were attached to his head with some duct tape, since they had no nose to sit on. He didn't look up when he spoke.

"What's all the racket out there? I can barely hear the radio." This was impressive, since the radio was quite loud.

Cooper stood up and leveled his pistol at the man. "Intruders," he said.

The man stopped typing and looked up. His dark black eyes widened. "Who are you?" he asked, then saw Pete standing in the door-frame behind Cooper, "And what are you doing with the Scribe?"

"I'm just a simple caravan merchant. I've got a delivery to make to a really persuasive customer, so I'm here to make a pickup."

"A...merchant?" The man in the medical coat blinked his eyes in confusion.

"The...the kid. The kid is the delivery. I was sent to rescue him, so I'm rescuing him and—look, whatever, do you have a bunch of prisoners behind that door?" Cooper motioned with his gun to a door behind the desk. A sign above it said "NO ADMITTANCE DURING TESTING."

"The converts? They are currently being processed. They cannot leave the room." There was another pained scream from behind the door.

"What are you doing to them?" Cooper asked.

The man kept his mouth firmly shut until Cooper cocked the pistol, then he reluctantly spoke. "Creating a future for the ghouls. This, along with the Book of Truth that the Scribe is transcribing, is Blake's great gift to our kind. Once transformed, they will be taught our ways, and the Church shall grow in number."

"Transformed?" Cooper asked.

"I'm sorry, but I have specific instructions for intruders." The man brought his hands out from under the desk and fired a shotgun at Cooper from point-blank range. Thankfully, right at the same moment, Pete tackled his legs and brought them both to the ground, the shot going over their heads. The man stood up and came around the desk, and Cooper fired from where he was on the ground, aiming for his torso. Pete covered his ears as the sharp cracks of Cooper's 10mm pistol rang out in the small room. The man fell back against the wall and slumped down it.

Cooper stood up and brushed himself off, turning to Pete. "You okay?" he asked. Pete nodded his head, but looked more pale than he had before. Cooper turned off the blaring radio and searched the man's pockets for keys, but didn't find any. He looked at the lock on the door, and found that it didn't have a traditional lock. Cooper scratched his head, then Pete spoke up, "Maybe the computer?"

Cooper looked at it and laughed nervously. "Oh, yeah. I can do computers. I'm very skilled at computers."

He was not. North Fork had one old computer, and it hadn't worked in years. Pete didn't need to know that, though. Cooper sat in the chair and looked at the terminal's screen. Green letters, stopped mid-sentence, described the most recent experiments the Church scientist had been performing. The entry the man had been typing read:

Batch 9 is progressing well. We expect to see a few survivors in the group who can then undergo education. The two subjects captured with the child are healthy and strong, and should make good candidates for the process. With the recent supply of FEV we acquired, we can renew our experiments immediately....

"Looks like they're here," Cooper said. "Now, just have to unlock this computer door." He searched the screen for some kind of unlock option, and clicked through a few menus until he came to an input screen. Cooper was aware of Pete watching him, and smiled confidently as he typed in UNLOCK DOOR. The terminal made a loud, negative-sounding beep and Cooper's smile fell. Pete walked over, waved him away, and clacked away at the keyboard until a different beep signaled the lock opening behind them.

Cooper pulled open the door, which was heavy and thick. The room was lined with six beds on either side, with the people lying in them attached to neon-yellow tubes and various diagnostic machines. As he looked down the room, Cooper realized that each successive row of beds contained people whose bodies were more scarred and decayed. One man was thrashing and pulling at his restraints wordlessly. Several weren't moving at all.

"Bryant! John!" Pete called out and ran to the bed closest to the door. The man there was covered in sweat, and looked exhausted. His skin was dark red in some places, but otherwise he looked normal. He rolled his head towards Pete and groggily spoke.

"Pete...? Pete you're alive...You have to..." He coughed. "Have to..."

Cooper felt the charge in the air before he heard anything. It was like something invisible was gathering towards the ceiling. A low, electrical buzzing sound was slowly getting louder, and Cooper noticed a domed light in the center of the room was starting to glow. The sound and light intensified until there was a sudden blinding flash. Cooper turned his back and hunched protectively over Pete, coat wrapped around him. The room was filled with a chorus of agonized screams and moans, which seemed to go on forever, despite it only being a few seconds before the mechanism could be heard winding down and the whirring subsided.

Cooper opened his eyes, and felt...incredible. All the weariness from his travels had been washed away, and his sore back actually felt better, too. Looking down, he saw that Pete had passed out. Worriedly, Cooper gently shook him. He didn't wake, but he did seem to be breathing.

"Radiation." The Boomer strapped to the bed next to them spoke up, his breathing heavy. "It...helps the virus...changes..." He broke into another coughing fit.

"Will Pete be alright?" Cooper asked.

"Need….RadAway...soon..."

"Alright, I'm getting you guys out of here." Cooper unbuckled the man's restraints and helped him stand. "I'm Cooper, by the way. Pearl sent me."

The man nodded, a bit shaky on his feet. "Bryant...That's John," he motioned to the other bed. They removed John's restraints and woke him up. The radiation and virus seemed to be affecting John more. His hair had fallen out in places, and Cooper could see bits of bone beneath the reddened skin. Yet, when he stood up, he seemed surer on his feet and less exhausted than Bryant. He picked Pete up off the ground and carried him in his arms.

"I'm going to release the rest of these people," Cooper said, somewhat surprising himself. "You take Pete and find a way out. Try not to get killed. Actually, do some killing if you can. It'd really help me out. Oh, and see if you can find Bockscar." The two men nodded at Cooper and ran out of the room. What kind of hero act is this? Cooper thought to himself as he moved to assist the half-dozen people who still looked alive.

A few of those Cooper released were already dead, but the ones who were conscious took Cooper's advice in leaving the Church behind. Once the last was out, Cooper went back out into the hallway. The doctor's shotgun was gone, probably picked up by one of the Boomers. Cooper reckoned this was the case—he had heard a shot fired from it after they left, and the computer had been aggressively shut down via a blast to the screen.

He couldn't hear any commotion outside any more, and wasn't sure if that was a good thing or not. With the radio off and no more explosions, the halls of the makeshift church-prison were eerily quiet. Cooper reloaded his pistol, grateful for the ammo he kept in his coat, and jogged off down the long, straight hallway, hoping there was some kind of an exit that way.

He followed it until he came out into a large, dark storage room. Unlike the others Cooper had passed during his pleasant welcome tour with Bertrand, which were mostly full of everyday supplies, this room was full of weapons of all shapes and sizes. Rifles, submachine guns, rocket launchers—the ghouls here were as well equipped, if not better, than the Boomers. It looked like Blake had a backup if his book failed to impress the world outside Los. Either that, or he planned to have some heavily supervised reading time.

Cooper saw an open door off to his right that opened

to the outside, and started to move towards the exit that would finally take him out of this ridiculous mess of a rescue when he heard the familiar lowing of a certain rusty red brahmin known to have a particular taste for Sugar Bombs.

"Pook!" Cooper shouted and scanned the room until he saw the herd shuffling nervously in the far corner of the storage room. Some of the packs were open and had been rummaged through, but the caravan looked otherwise unharmed. Cooper ran over to Pook and gave both heads a vigorous scratch, looking over the rest of the herd with joy.

"I'm definitely glad to see you, Pook. Let's get the hell out of this Deathclaw nest." Cooper went to buckle up the opened packs and lead the brahmin towards the open door.

"You will be going nowhere, traitorous, deceitful heretic!" Blake's voice boomed from across the room and the lights flashed on. He was alone, standing with his spear planted in the ground, and he looked furious.

He had come in from outside, and slammed the door behind him with a thunderous boom that shook Cooper's bones. He began to pace from side to side, "*The man who never alters his opinions is like standing water, and breeds reptiles of the mind.* How is it that you cannot see the truth of the cause?" Blake pointed the long tip of his bladed spear towards Cooper, who flinched, despite being on the other side of the room.

Cooper reached into a nearby pack and pulled out two of Joshua Graham's .45s, silently thankful that he'd cleaned and loaded them during one of his nights by the fire. He checked the chambers, then slid them closed, standing as straight as he could.

Beneath the anger, Blake actually sounded hurt. "You would attack me? You would stand in the way of the blessed work we are doing here?"

"I've seen the prisoners, the experiments. Why are you making new ghouls? I thought you were all about helping ghouls make the best of a bad fate, not forcing innocent people to become them!" Cooper was taking deep breaths to try and steady his hands, but even standing on the other side of the room, Blake's size and strength were imposing, and being stuck in an enclosed space with him would mean that Cooper had nowhere to run.

"Our kind does not reproduce. We rot away and die while the plague that is man breeds and spreads across the land unheeded—greedily consuming and claiming it as their own. It is an injustice of nature that we will overcome, taking our place as gods of this new world." Blake swung his spear in a wide arc.

Still out of range, Cooper stepped back. "You're just kidnapping people and blasting them with radiation! There's no way that actually works!"

"Thankfully, we have a failed experiment of some smoothskin scientists that we have changed and recreated in order to foster this new race of ghoul-kind. A program they were testing—what you call 116."

Cooper's eyes widened, his breath stopped short, and the pistols fell limply to his sides. "What?" he asked, stunned.

"Even the lowly creature that is man could see that ghouls were superior—we have less need for food and rest, we live for centuries, and where man is weakened by the radioactive poisons of the Great War, we *thrive*! Naturally, a group seeking power sought to control and utilize this. They took in refugees from small settlements that had suffered Raider attacks. Promised them aid. Women, children, anyone they found. Do you not see man's insatiable greed?" In a burst of anger, Blake swept his spear into some nearby shelves, breaking the metal supports and sending boxes of ammunition scattering across the floor.

Blake continued, "Over hundreds of trials, they found a combination of the Forced Evolutionary Virus and timed blasts of radiation that could produce ghouls that didn't immediately expire or turn feral. Even better, they had little memory of their lives before. The perfect clean slate for the corrupt government of man to weaponize and enslave."

Cooper shook his head. "I thought you said 116 was a weapon to kill ghouls, not create them." This was getting to be too much for Cooper to understand, and he was already way deeper than he wanted to be. He just came for the kid.

"An added benefit." Blake shrugged his massive shoulders. "Exposure to 116 was fatal for those who were already ghouls. Over time, it decayed them even further, and it spread from ghoul to ghoul. Useful for wiping out cells of resistance and ensuring that only the obedient ghouls they had created remained."

"How do you know all this?" Cooper asked.

"Because I was there. I witnessed the atrocities myself, and when the lab was destroyed in an attack by the Brotherhood of Steel, I was left to die. The accident overexposed me to the FEV and created the powerful form you see before you." Yet, I would have died in the rubble that day had I not been rescued by a passing ghoul. A ghoul who led a caravan." Blake flashed his teeth at Cooper in a wide grin.

"You were rescued by a ghoul…leading a caravan?" The thoughts in Cooper's head were wearily paddling in deep, dark water, with a large shape looming underneath.

"In that one gesture, that ghoul had done more for me than the whole of mankind ever had! He risked his life and pulled me to safety, along with one other. A child." Blake held out his open hand to Cooper, his voice again taking on that sermon-like quality, "*In the universe, there are things that are known, and things that are unknown, and in between, there are doors.* Open your mind to the doors of perception, Cooper, and know the truth."

The pistols slowly dropped from his hands and clattered to the ground. Suddenly Cooper remembered the dreams he had often had, of hospital beds and crawling flames. Of walls caving in around him. Of gentle, scarred hands lifting him up. He thought about the lack of other ghoul children in North Fork. He remembered asking his father what his birthday was

151

and being told he could pick whichever day he liked. He thought about how little they talked about his past, or his mother.

"Ghouls aren't born; they're created," Blake spoke, breaking into the memories that were rushing up to the surface of Cooper's mind. "And because of that, the world has nothing for them. We have to protect each other—"

"And lift each other up," Cooper finished, his mouth hanging open in disbelief. "My father says that. He…?"

"Saved the both of us that day, yes. And I believe that he did so for a greater purpose. To create beauty and power out of tragedy and despair. To deny this world that has nothing for us and change it to be *for* us."

"That's not what he would have wanted! It's evil! My father always wanted peace, not murder!" Cooper yelled, sounding very young even to his own ears.

"*Active Evil is better than Passive Good.* He did not go

far enough with his hidden 'community.' It is not enough to create one place where we can live, cowering in the shadows. Why should we not claim this world? I say it is ours, and I will take it! I will stop anyone who defies that dream of Paradise! Now, do you stand with us? Or against us? Tell me where the human child has gone." Blake readied his spear in front of him, and his eyes, piercing white, bored into Cooper's from beneath his hood.

Cooper thought about the people he'd met and places he'd seen since leaving the walls of Zion Canyon. Everyone from the Dead Horses to the Boomers, the family traveling together, even the Legionaries who had ridden with him—Cooper had imagined that, when he left North Fork, all he would find was hatred and fear, but what he had really seen in the Wasteland were people trying to survive and carve out some kind of happiness in a harsh world. Some people had tried to kill him, sure, but usually to protect what little they had, or to fight for something they believed in. Could

Cooper really stand by and let Blake and the Church of the Lost take those lives away and force them to change into something else? Could he support that? Let it continue after the things he'd learned and experienced thanks to all the different people in the world? He thought about the horrors that Two-Bears and his father had described about war between the tribes, vying for solitary control. He tried to imagine what his father would do, and wasn't sure if Blake was right that this is what he would want. He wasn't sure he knew as much about his father as he thought he did, but Cooper needed to make his own decision, and be in control of his own story.

"Thanks for the invitation," he started, edging back closer to the caravan, "but I'm not one of your Lost, and I'm not going to help you force anyone else to be."

As Blake shouted in rage and began to run towards him, Cooper pulled the Fat Man out of its bag and launched the mini-nuke straight at Blake's chest. There was a blinding flash, and Cooper dove for cover behind a stack of iron crates, shielding his face and head with his arms. He heard a shocked howl of pain and rage as the explosion engulfed Blake's body and ignited the munitions he had knocked to the ground. Underneath the rushing sound of air from the localized nuclear detonation, there were pops, cracks, and the sounds of the building starting to collapse as a corner of it ceased to exist.

As it cleared, Cooper stood up, ears still ringing, and squinted at the exit door. He couldn't see or hear anything, but knew he needed to get out. The side of the room Blake had been standing in was clouded in heavy smoke and dust from the rubble that had been the outer wall. Cooper set the Fat Man down, and turned around to check on the herd, who were as docile as ever in the face of combat. He picked up the .45s he had dropped, then cautiously made his way over to check Blake's body, holding the pistols in front of him like a shield. There was no way that even the enormous, enraged ghoul could have survived all that.

It was the most powerful weapon he'd ever seen.

Cooper took a few steps into the smoke and saw a pile of shelves and debris in the haze. He started to wonder if there was anything left of Blake under all that when a heavy blow smashed into his chest like a charging Bighorner and knocked him across the room. He landed hard and slid a few feet, gasping for breath. He tried to roll onto his back, reaching out for one of the guns that had been knocked from his hands, when a cold, searing pain burrowed itself deep into his left shoulder. Cooper cried out, and felt himself being slowly and agonizingly lifted into the air by the spear he was now skewered on. Blake's voice came from somewhere on the other end.

"I wander thro' each charter'd street, Near where the charter'd Thames does flow, And mark in every face I meet Marks of weakness, marks of woe. In every cry of every Man, In every Infant's cry of fear, In every voice, in every ban, The mind-forg'd manacles I hear. How the Chimney-sweeper's cry Every black'ning Church appalls;

And the hapless Soldier's sigh Runs in blood down Palace walls. But most thro' midnight streets I hear How the youthful Harlot's curse Blasts the newborn Infant's tear, And blights with plagues the Marriage hearse."

The smoke was clearing, and he could see a bloodied Blake holding the spear, somehow standing on ruined feet that were little more than ragged stumps. The shot from the Fat Man must have hit him low. Cooper cursed himself for thinking a 3-pound round would travel straight without any drop. Blake's hood had fallen back, and Cooper could take in the complete, crazed expression of his near-skeletal face. Blood was running down his face and into his eyes, and the blast had stripped much of his flesh off, exposing open bone all along his body.

"You would throw away our future? Act to save *smoothskins?* Turn against your own kind?" Blake shook the spear and the movement set off horrible, fresh waves of pain that washed over Cooper's body and muddled his vision as he felt himself being dragged into unconsciousness. His breathing was rough, and it was difficult to slow it down, but he tried to focus. He flexed his right hand and found it could move. Fighting the black current trying to pull him under, he reached into his pocket and found his father's pistol. It was almost too heavy for him to lift. Another deep breath. Blake was yelling, but he couldn't hear him now. There was only the target, and his father's words: *fight to make it home.*

He fired, and the bullet struck square between Blake's blood-red eyes, the anger and hate draining until the life was gone behind them. He collapsed to the ground, and Cooper fell hard on his side, still impaled on the spear. He reached out his still-working right hand to look for something to pull him up and felt the hilt of the Fat Man. Groaning, and losing blood, he put it between his knees, and with some effort chambered the next round. He didn't know if he was going to make it home, but he hoped Pete and the others would, and he was going to make sure that no one else got abducted to join Blake's stupid ghoul army.

With pain shooting through his entire left side like jolts of electricity from a bad wire, he swung the Fat Man's barrel to point down the long hallway that led back to the labs and the main hall. His arms were shaking, and his labored breathing was getting slower, so he knew he had to be quick. Gritting his teeth against the pain and blackness pressing in on his vision, he squeezed the trigger and the remaining mini-nuke flew out of the barrel with enough force to spin Cooper 90 degrees on the floor. The round skated above the ground, finally detonating against the corner next to the lab. Cooper could feel the force of the blast through the ground as he lay there.

"Good," he said. "Good."

The last thing he saw before finally succumbing to the inky darkness closing in on his vision was Pook standing over him, one head nudging his hand, the other licking his face. He closed his eyes, and thought of his father's workshop. He could hear him singing along to his favorite song on the radio.

I've wrangled, and I've rambled, and I've rodeoed around

I've never once thought of settling down

But darling, the moment I laid eyes on you

I knew my ramblin' days were through

Made up my mind a long time ago

When the right man came along, somehow I'd know

Heart as true, eyes as blue, and his smile as wide

As a western sky

Let's ride into the sunset together

Stirrup to stirrup, side by side

When the day is through, I'll be here with you

Into the sunset we will ride

VIII. The End

"You reckon this is a good idea, Pete?"

"He risked his life for us. He shouldn't be a prisoner."

A sort of plodding, bumpy movement underneath him was gradually jostling Cooper back into the waking world—mostly because it was making his left-shoulder feel like it was being scorched by Fire Ants. He opened his eyes, and saw he was on Pook's back, thrown over like a sack of feed. Standing in front of him were the two Boomers and Pete.

"Well, this seems familiar," Cooper said from his awkward hanging position.

The Boomers didn't hear him and continued working. The motion that had woken him up was Bryant fiddling with the iron cuff around his left arm while Pete looked on. There was a click, and Cooper braced himself, half-expecting to be blown up, but the contraption merely fell to the ground. He looked at it for a moment, then let out the breath he had been holding.

"Thanks," he said to Pete, a little louder this time.

"It only seemed fair," Pete replied, seemingly unsurprised by his awakening.

"You look a lot better," Cooper said, noticing the boy had most of his color back. "Also, conscious. That's good." Pete smiled at him.

"We used some of the RadAway you had," explained Bryant. "Paid for it, too, in case you were worried. Put some caps in your money bag there."

Cooper looked back to see the rest of the caravan was there, which was also the exact moment he realized he was supposed to be dead. The Boomers explained that, when Pete saw the explosions light up the night sky at the Church, he ran back. Apparently they found Cooper surrounded by the brahmin, who had protectively circled around him, and were hearty enough to be unharmed by a few roof tiles and some concrete collapsing on top of them.

"You were lucky you were in one of the rooms towards the outside so we could get to you," Pete said.

"What about the rest of the Church?" Cooper asked.

"Rubble," said Pete. "Most of the ghouls had already run out when Bockscar attacked the guards, and the rest did when they heard the first explosion."

"Didn't give us any trouble," said Bryant. "Most of 'em just stood around, looking like they were..."

"Lost," Cooper finished. "Well, whatever they do now isn't my problem. I still need to find a cure for 116, and I kind of forgot when I was blowing it up that the Church might have had some clue as to how to do that."

"Oh, just a moment," said Pete, digging around in one

of the packs. He pulled out a thin, gray box. "Computer expert that you are, I'm sure you know what this is?"

"Sure, but explain it for these guys," said Cooper, grimacing in pain as he tried to reposition himself on Pook's back.

"Before we left the lab, I copied the computer onto this holotape. I thought it might be important, and saving important records is what a Keeper is supposed to do. It might have some information about 116 that you can use."

In his surprise, Cooper slid off Pook's back, managing to land on his non-injured shoulder. The Boomers helped him stand, and he took the holotape from Pete.

"Thank you, Pete. I just hope I can get back in time. Where are we, anyway?"

"Waiting to be picked up," Pete said, pointing to the sky. Cooper looked up just in time to see some enormous flying machine swoop low overhead and circle back. In the glare of its massive floodlights, Cooper noticed that they were standing on a wide, flat, paved surface.

"What the hell is that thing?" Cooper shouted over the noise of the landing.

"The Pearl! Our Boeing B-29 Superfortress!" Pete shouted back.

When it finally came to a stop, Cooper, Pete, the Boomers, and the six Brahmin all walked across the tarmac. Cooper had seen NCR vertibirds passing overhead before, and looked at pictures of airplanes in some comic books, but never one that was working, and never one this impressively large. Near the cockpit, there was a painted picture of a beautiful young woman, posing in a Vault 34 jumpsuit like he'd seen some of the Boomers wearing under their leather jackets. Painted above her was the name Pearl. Cooper raised an eyebrow at it before leading the caravan onto a ramp that had dropped from the underside of the plane. Standing at the top of the ramp was the real

Pearl, looking considerably more wrinkled than the cartoon version on the hull, but just as happy. She embraced Pete in a tight hug, and greeted Cooper as he walked up.

"You asked to be flown home, didn't you?" She smiled. "You have done us an incredible service, my child. You have protected that which is most important and precious to us and brought our Keeper home. We will not forget this, and we will do everything we can to help you."

Cooper held up the holotape with the information about 116. "I hope you're as good at medical research as you are at explosives."

"Perhaps not, but we may have found some who are."

Cooper looked out over Zion Canyon as the morning sun was rising. In just a few more hours, he'd finally be home. It had been almost a month since Cooper destroyed the Church of the Lost. After riding back to the Boomer's base, Cooper had been introduced to three scientists, one of which was a ghoul who called himself Barrows. He had tagged along with the two New Canaanites, saying that his "hobby" was researching ways to slow the ghoulification process, when he wasn't busy acting as mayor of Underworld. Over the weeks, Barrow made a lot of dry, sarcastic jokes, so Cooper never did learn how true that was.

They had poured over the data from the holotape Pete took, and ran test after test on Cooper to see why he was immune, hypothesizing that it had something to do with him having been made into a ghoul through 116 exposure as a child. They worked day and night, fueled by curiosity and the Boomers' energizing tea. Cooper didn't understand most of the conversations that were happening, but could never bring himself to leave the room where they were working, maybe thinking that somehow his presence and good wishes would engender some miracle breakthrough.

Whether it was that, or three sharp scientific minds

motivated partially by fear of a heavily armed group insisting on their success, late one night Barrows jostled Cooper awake and confidently announced that they had a vaccine that should halt the rapid degeneration that 116 was causing in the ghouls at North Fork. Without wasting any time, Cooper loaded it into the caravan, which was fully stocked with fresh supplies (Pearl had also made good on Cooper's half-joking request to buy his stock at twice the price). Cooper had set out that same morning, moving the brahmin as fast as they would go, stopping only for water.

And now he was back home. He only hoped he wasn't too late. He whistled for the caravan to move down the winding path into the canyon. They seemed eager, as if they could also sense how close the end was. When they were in sight of the cave entrance leading to North Fork a few hours later, Cooper grabbed the box containing the vaccines and began to sprint towards home. The brahmin knew the way from here, and could make their own way back.

Cooper ran through the entrance and into the main hall, giving his eyes no time to adjust. He tripped over some chairs and nearly fell, cradling the box closely to his chest. The clamor was terribly loud in the still, silent hall. For some reason, all the tables and chairs had been pushed towards the front to make room for something. Dr. Tremain's door opened and he looked around. When he saw Cooper, he ran over to him and took him by the shoulders, looking him up and down.

"Cooper! Sure took your time, kid. I was starting to fear the worst." He broke into a coughing fit that shook his body.

The words came tumbling out of Cooper's mouth as he was trying to catch his breath from the run, "Dr. Tremain, I have the cure—the cure for 116—I got kidnapped but then I found a computer in the Church of the Lost where they were doing experiments and we brought the holotape to Dr. Barrows and the New Canaanites and they think they found a cure—is my dad here? Am I in time? Did I make it?"

Dr. Tremain was already leading him towards his office, still coughing, "Tom's still breathing. Always the fighter, but he's barely holding on. More have fallen sick—including me, actually. Let's hope this cure works, or else this town will get very lonely for you." His chuckles broke into more coughs.

Beds had been pulled from homes around North Fork, and had spilled out of Dr. Tremain's office and into the main hall. It looked like the entire surviving population of the town was bedridden, and Cooper could hear people talking and calling out to him as they rushed to his father's bedside. Tremain wasted no time in preparing the vaccine as Cooper leaned over his father, who looked smaller and somehow less substantial—barely there, like a ghost clinging to life. His breathing was shallow and quiet.

"I'm here, dad. I'm home," Cooper said, placing a hand on his father's. "Just hold on."

Dr. Tremain gently injected the needle into his father's

arm, then stood back. "We'll have to wait and see," he said. "I'm going to vaccinate myself and then work on the others. Let's hope we're all still here in the morning." He shuffled off, leaving Cooper sitting at his father's side.

"Come back home, dad. Come back home." Cooper repeated it over and over as he sat there, exhaustion eventually dragging him into an uneasy sleep.

In his dreams, Cooper was back on the B-29, flying above the Mojave Wasteland. He looked out over the red desert, patched with thickets of harsh vegetation, criss-crossed with broken roads and dirty rivers, rising and falling with the rolling hills and jutting plateaus. He moved through the plane, realizing that it looked a lot like the home he'd grown up in. There was the old, battered sofa. There was the faded Dean Domino poster. There was his stack of comics and dog-eared mechanics magazines. He walked up to the door leading to the engine room, and it was the door to his father's workshop. Behind the door, someone was humming. Cooper pushed open the door, and saw his father bent over the plane's massive engine, tinkering away.

"Give me a hand, Cooper," the dream-father said, motioning him over as he always did. "It's up to us to keep this whole thing running."

Cooper knelt down next to him and took the wrench he was being offered. As soon as it was in his hands, though, the wrench became a pistol, matted red with blood. Cooper tried to drop it, but couldn't let it go.

"I—I can't help you, dad. I don't remember...I can only..." his own voice sounded far away and fake, like a recording.

"Sure you do, son. That gun is not the only tool we have. You can use it to fix, or break. To build, or destroy. To save, or to hurt. It can't do everything, and when you come home, you put it away. You *have* to put it away." His father placed the wrench he was holding into Cooper's other hand. Cooper looked at them both there, and gripped the wrench tightly to keep it from changing. His father was looking at him, and his face seemed to be moving and shifting. "Do you understand, Cooper?"

Cooper?

...Cooper...

...Cooper...

...Cooper...

Cooper jolted awake. He had been leaning on his left side while sleeping, and it ached in protest. For a moment, he couldn't remember where he was, and looked around the dark medical office. It was a small, weak voice next to him that snapped him into reality.

"Cooper..." his father's voice was just above a whisper, but it was real.

"Dad! Yes, yes, I'm here! Are you—" Cooper began to ask.

"Cooper, please..." his father found his hand and

grabbed it.

"What is it? Tell me. Anything. I'll—"

"Turn on the radio...it's, so quiet in here...it's been so...goddamn boring…" Cooper must have looked as surprised as he felt, because Thomas Pulman laughed as much as a man coming out of a near-fatal super plague could. Cooper joined him, and when he turned on the radio, he felt like he was well and truly back home, and that things would be alright.

For a while, he could forget the Wasteland, and who he was out there. He could put all that down, at least for now, until it was time to venture out once again. There'd be time for stories and questions later. For now, he brought the radio over to his father's bedside, so they could sing together in low, raspy voices without waking up the rest of the recovering town.

The food is the spreadiest, the wine is the headiest

The pals are the readiest, the gals are the steadiest

The love the liveliest, the life the loveliest

Way back, way back, way back home

No place like home

Sweet home

COMPLETED: Cooper's Caravan